D0277246

EYE

ON

Also by Robert Westall

The Making of Me
A Writer's Childhood
Edited by Lindy McKinnel

The WIND EYE

Robert Westall

CATNIP BOOKS
Published by Catnip Publishing Ltd.
Islington Business Centre
3-5 Islington High Street
London N1 9LQ

This edition published 2007
1 3 5 7 9 10 8 6 4 2

A CIP catalogue record for this book is available from the British Library

ISBN 10: 1 84647 028 5
ISBN 13: 978-1-84647-028-8

Printed in Poland

www.catnippublishing.co.uk

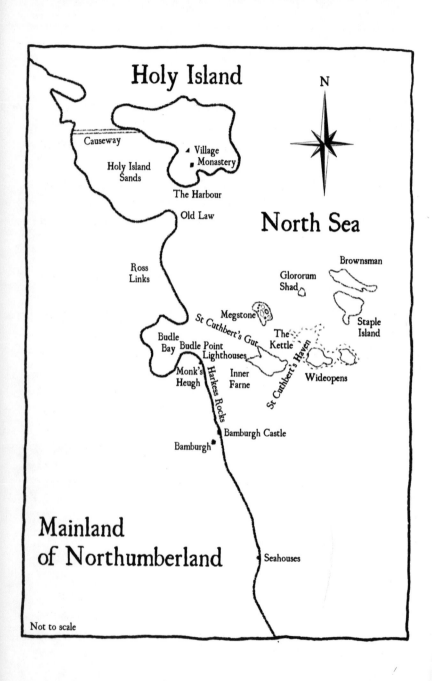

I

When they were all ready, and in the dining-room, Professor Bertrand Studdard made his expected plea for sanity.

"Why don't you come with us in the Volvo?" he asked in a hopeless voice.

Madeleine pretended to pause and think; until hope dawned on her husband's face. Then she said: "The Volvo? *That* thing? It's more like a bus than a car, and you drive it like a bus-driver."

"You can drive, if you like …"

"I wouldn't be seen dead in it. Besides, the clutch makes my leg ache."

The three children watched silently. Could this family never do anything without a row? thought Beth. Could they never go on holiday in one car, like other families? Heavens, the Volvo was big enough!

"I'm sorry," said Madeleine, in a voice that wasn't sorry at all. "I'm sorry, but I like to feel *free* when I drive. See you at Durham." She pulled on her black driving-gloves, the ones with round holes in the back, and swept out. The others stood silently till the front door slammed, and the Triumph Spitfire started up in the drive. It made a very rude noise that died slowly away.

"See you in Durham," echoed Michael bitterly. "We should be so lucky. She'll be on our tails in ten miles."

"Don't be rude about your mother," said Bertrand automatically.

"She's *my* mother," shouted Michael. "Just because you've married her doesn't stop me saying what I think. I said things like that before you even knew her!"

The two males glared at each other.

Beth said quickly, "Please don't fight. We've got a long way to go."

"Oh, all right," said Michael ungraciously. "Sorry, Bertrand. Didn't mean to get narky with *you* – you're O.K."

"Thanks," said Bertrand sarcastically, but you could tell he was pleased.

"But Mother gets my goat …"

"Michael …"

"Oh, O.K. Let's go."

They cheered up by the time they reached the A1(M). There was no doubt it was more peaceful driving with Bertrand on his own. His hands made little soothing motions on gearstick and wheel and the Volvo seemed to drive itself. Also Bertrand had time to talk.

"There's another kestrel."

"That's the third we've seen. Why are there so many on motorways?" asked Beth.

"Think it out for yourself."

Beth groaned inwardly. She hated her father's thinking-competitions.

"There's a chocolate for the first one who gets it," added Bertrand.

From behind, Michael was first into the act.

"The cars on the motorway make hot air, and it helps the kestrel fly."

"Intelligent, but wrong," said Bertrand. Then he said to himself, "Though I wonder … it might be a subsidiary factor. I'll ask old George Thompson … he'll know. Meanwhile, a chocolate for the bright gent on the back seat." His hand moved to the glove compartment, he flicked, and a chocolate went flying backwards through the air. Michael caught it.

"Well taken," said Bertrand. "You'll make a scrum-half yet."

"I am – for the school," said Michael with his mouth full.

"I stand corrected," said Bertrand. "Come on, Beth, what's

the answer about the kestrels? Are they just doing it for laughs?"

Beth's chest tightened with shame. She couldn't think at all.

"Well, what are kestrels *looking* for?" said Bertrand patiently as if she was one of his duller students.

"Food, I suppose …"

"*What* food?" Bertrand would not leave her alone till he got the answer.

"Little animals, I suppose."

"Ye—es?"

"And there are lots of little animals on the motorway verges because they get killed …"

"And … ?"

"Because a lot live there; because there are no men and dogs …"

"Good girl," said Bertrand warmly. "Chocolate for the bright lady in the front seat." Beth blushed with pleasure; but underneath she knew she wasn't as bright as Bertrand wanted her to be.

However, Bertrand had moved on, because the third child in the car hadn't had a chocolate yet, and the third was only six.

"Sally?"

"Mmmmm?" Without turning round, Beth could tell that Sally was sucking her thumb.

"Sally, what's another name for a kestrel?"

"Windhover," said Sally, relieved. Beth heard Michael unwrap the chocolate for her.

"What a bright family I have," said Bertrand, and began whistling a sixteenth-century madrigal with great precision.

The whole car felt happy, till Michael suddenly said, "Here she comes – right on time." Bertrand glanced in the rear mirror. The three children stared stonily out of the back window. A small red dot was approaching at alarming speed, though the Volvo was doing sixty.

"She's doing a ton," said Michael. "Big deal." Then he added "Oh, Jesus, look at that!"

The Spitfire had hurled itself into the narrowing gap where an articulated truck was moving out into the fast lane. Then, with a burst of blue exhaust from its overdriven engine, the little red car snatched itself free of the grinding juggernaut. They could see Madeleine leaning over to shake her fist at the truck-driver, while her front wheels wobbled dangerously.

"She's on her third gearbox this year," said Michael, bitter with relief.

Beth watched her father's hands tighten on the steering-column. Why on earth had he married Madeleine? Anyone could see she had only wanted an affair.

Bertrand had met her at a party; one of the few he ever attended. Three days later, Madeleine turned up dripping-wet on the doorstep, with an urgent problem about car insurance. Bertrand solved it with one phonecall. The admiring Madeleine stayed for a drink.

After that, there was a succession of small problems; and drinks. Bertrand held forth to his daughters about the strains of one-parent families …

One night late, Madeleine had lingered a long time laughing by the front door. Next morning she came down for breakfast as cool as a cucumber.

Beth had been sorely puzzled. Father Wilson, the Vicar, always preached that affairs were wrong; the Permissive Society was ruining the country. But it was good to see her father laughing again; buying new suits, and curtains for the kitchen. Madeleine had been fun too, cooking sausages by firelight on a Suffolk beach; imitating the giraffe for Sally on the trip to Whipsnade. She had a quick dancing mind and no academic training. It was fun, watching Bertrand trying to teach her to argue logically. She always wriggled through his fingers.

Then the gossip started …

Cambridge was broader-minded than it used to be, but Bertrand wasn't. Having spent years advocating Free Love in theory, he was uneasy being caught practising it.

There was a week of desperate gloom, which ended with Madeleine packing her bags and leaving Cambridge. Three days later she was back on the doorstep, eyes beautiful with tears …

A quick furtive marriage in the registry-office and the trouble really started. Bertrand began talking about *my* wife, as he had always talked about *my* daughters and *my* house. The gay logical arguments turned into screaming-matches, as Bertrand strove to tidy up Madeleine's life, and Madeleine resisted with increasing wildness.

They only agreed when they were criticising other people. Sometimes, late at night, there would be laughter coming from their bedroom. But it seemed to Beth that they only stayed together to prove each other wrong. And because if one of them left it would be an admission of defeat.

Damn people like Father Wilson … no affair could have caused such misery.

But then it *was* nice having Mike as one of the family … oh, she was in one of her muddles again …

And there was no time to get it straight now. Madeleine was right on their tail, almost touching their bumper-bar. She was mouthing words and making gestures, and it was all too clear what she wanted.

Madeleine was lonely; Madeleine wanted company. Madeleine wanted a child to map-read for her, even though it was motorway all the way to Durham.

The children exchanged grim looks. They all loathed driving with Madeleine. She drove well enough, otherwise she would never have survived her thirty-six years. But she drove with drama. As Michael said, her car might as well have been the other kind of Spitfire, in the Battle of Britain.

When she pursued a petrol-tanker (her favourite prey) you could almost hear the machine-guns firing.

Then there was her non-stop running commentary on her foes. "Just look at *that* bloody idiot, will you? Get over, get over, you fool. The man's a lunatic. He ought to be certified. Put a man in a car, and what have you got – a killer!"

Madeleine continued to hang on the bumper-bar. She began sounding her horn. She would go on doing it until she got her way.

The only child who was safe was Sally. Sally had stated, the first time Madeleine asked her, that driving in the Spitfire would make her sick. Madeleine had insisted. Sally had been gorgeously sick, all down Madeleine's purple trouser-suit. She had never been asked again. But Sally could get away with it, because she was six. Michael and Beth were teenagers and teenagers were not expected to be sick.

Michael took the brunt of it, because he was Madeleine's son. He was no coward; even had a streak of his mother's recklessness. But he sometimes looked so pale and shaken that Beth went instead. She usually shut her eyes and prayed, but that *really* made you feel sick.

Bertrand knew how they felt. He ignored Madeleine's fuss as long as possible. But then she came alongside to argue, doing only sixty in the fast lane. A hooting queue of vehicles grew behind her. Bertrand surrendered and pulled into a service station.

Madeleine came across, furious.

"Are you all blind? You could see I wanted something. I *am* part of this family, you know." Everyone bit back a sarky remark except Sally, who simply said: "I feel sick."

"You poor darling," cooed Madeleine. "It's sitting in the back of the Bus that's making you sick." Her syrupy tones set Beth's teeth on edge. Sally began sucking her thumb again. The thumb of her bad hand. That always made things tense.

"Oh, I'll come with you," said Michael abruptly.

"How gracious," said his mother. "That *really* makes me feel wanted. I wonder you aren't all bored stiff, sitting in the back of that Bus."

"Let's get moving," said Bertrand, starting his engine. They watched the red car vanish in the distance, hanging dangerously close to the back of a removal van, nipping in and out.

Half-an-hour later, Beth saw it speeding in the opposite direction, down the southbound carriageway. Madeleine was playing her game of flyover-bridges again.

"Poor Michael!"

"Don't be rude about your stepmother," said Bertrand automatically. But he added, "You two stay with me today. This is a Bad Day." They were silent; they knew what a Bad Day meant.

II

Beth was glad to stop at Durham. Sally had sung her interminable car-song for the last hundred and fifty miles, in between sucking the thumb of her bad hand.

It was peaceful. The lunchtime sun was directly over the cathedral tower, making you squint. White doves were fluttering out of the black belfry. Below, pairs of unisex students held hands.

It was peaceful till Madeleine arrived, with the usual screech of brakes and scrunch of gravel; slewing sideways so she took up two parking-places instead of one.

Madeleine got out, showing a lot of elegant leg. She stood poised by the sports-car's bonnet, one hand raised, watching the doves. She made a beautiful romantic picture with her long black hair; until you realised she was deliberately posing to make a romantic picture. Then you noticed her waist was getting a bit thick.

God, I am a cat, thought Beth. Why do I hate her so much? Father Wilson said it was wrong ever to hate. But she couldn't love Madeleine, or even like her, no matter how much she tried, and that was guilty-making.

Bertrand locked the car-door carefully, and said, "Lunch," in a calm voice. "I'm told the Talbot Arms do you well."

"Christ," said Madeleine, "I can just imagine it. Brown Windsor soup. Beef and two veg. Tinned fruit and tinned milk. Half-cold coffee. You're getting so *bourgeois*, Bertrand." Bertrand went white; he hated being called bourgeois more than anything.

"What do you suggest then?"

Madeleine's eyes roamed the cathedral square and came to rest on a snack-bar, its windows obscured with lemonade adverts and steam.

"*That* looks interesting. Where *real* people eat; people who work with their *hands*. Come on, it'll stop you all turning into a pack of snobs."

Beth and Michael groaned loudly. Sally said, "I *like* Brown Windsor soup." But Madeleine was already on her way. It was either follow her or provoke a real row; in public. It was a very Bad Day.

The snack-bar was awful. The red plastic tables were so close together you couldn't breathe, and a deafening juke-box played last month's Top-of-the-Pops. The sauce-bottles had stalactites. The meat pies were lukewarm.

But Madeleine hadn't come for the food. She was watching a group of workmen in the corner.

"Stone-masons from the cathedral," she announced.

"Steady on," said Bertrand. But he was too late; she was among them. The way she leaned over their table caused much interest among the other customers. Everyone stopped eating when she spoke; she had that sort of voice.

"Are you working on the cathedral?"

"No, hinny," said a bald man, "me and Ben here's on the dust-carts."

"But surely *one* of you works on the cathedral?"

"George here does – bin a mason forty year."

"There – I knew it! What are you working on – a new gargoyle?"

"Well, no." George was a dry old stick. He suddenly remembered to take off his cap and twisted it between his hands, embarrassed. "No hinny – we've been mekking good the foondations, the last twelve-month."

"But *surely* you have carved a gargoyle some time?"

Beth hated Madeleine's but-surely voice; people who didn't come up to expectation suffered.

"Well, aah carved a little one, once."

"Show me." She seized the old man by the arm.

"Foreman will be mad if I'm back late for work."

"Steady on, Madeleine," said Bertrand again. But the other old men were egging George on.

"Go on, George – you've clicked. She's a right smasher."

So a little procession wound across the cathedral square. Madeleine held the old man's elbow and talked non-stop. The family trailed behind in silence. The other men brought up the rear, whispering and laughing.

George showed them his gargoyle. It was so high on the roof, it was nearly invisible. But that didn't stop Madeleine having opinions about it.

Then she insisted on a conducted tour inside the cathedral with George on one side of her, and Bertrand on the other. She made fools of them alternately. She used long words to the old man which he couldn't understand, like "tympanum" and "iconography". She taunted Bertrand by talking about the Faith of the Middle Ages and the Glory of God, which made Bertrand writhe. What was more, Beth noticed, she was setting one man against the other.

After a bit, the other workmen slunk off, muttering, "Stuck-up little cow, i'nt she?"

Beth wanted to agree out loud. Instead she drifted away into the quiet dark of the side-aisles, where tattered flags hung and stone bishops lay on their backs, staring at the ceiling. Marble cherubs flew with dust-laden wings, and there were little dim memorials you had to peer at. But their message was always the same; the dead cried:

"Remember me; remember me!"

So many wanting to be remembered; and only Beth to remember them. At first she enjoyed it, in a sad way; and then suddenly there were too many of them. Their weight dragged her down; she fled back to her family.

Up in the Chapel of Nine Altars, old George was mumbling worse than ever, and Madeleine was still telling him what he *ought* to be saying.

Then Beth heard George's voice turn sharp.

"Watch where you're walking, hinny!"

Everyone looked. Set in the floor, between tall silver candlesticks, was a black slab carrying one word.

CUTHBERTUS

"That's Cuddy doon there," said the old mason. His voice trembled.

"Cuddy? You call St Cuthbert Cuddy? How *very* quaint." Madeleine was overcome with delight at this living folk-lore.

"Aye, and us masons know too much to mess wi' him. Ye knaa, when his tomb was built, the Prior and the Monks didn't knaa what te carve on it. They bickered and bickered, while us masons waited. Then one day, Cuddy settled the matter himself. Two masons fell asleep beside the slab. When they wekkened up, the name had been carved for them, just as you see it today."

Madeleine clapped her hands.

"A *miracle*! What do you say to that, Bertrand?" That rattled Bertrand, made him sharp with the old man. Beth could have cried because Bertrand tried so hard to be tolerant to everybody.

"When did this happen? Were you here then?"

The old man flinched.

"Wey, no, mister. It wes hundreds o' years ago."

"Is there contemporary documentary evidence?"

"Don't knaa what ye mean, mister."

"Then you shouldn't talk superstitious rubbish."

Now the old mason was angry; his pale watery eyes blazed.

"Don't talk to me with your long words. Aah divent know long words, but aah do know Cuddy. So you better watch how you talk where he can hear. Years ago, there was a scarlet wumman in this town, who plied her trade wi' those high enough to know better. She swore she'd touch Cuddy's tomb, cos she know'd he couldn't stomach a wumman. But Prior and Monks were here then, an' they kept her at bay. But when King Henry done away wi' the monks, this wumman was first into the church. She touched this tomb and ses 'Aye, Cuddy, aah has ye now!' And at that very minute, a great lump o' the roof brek off, and fell doon, missing her by a hair's breadth. She tuk to her heels and wes never seen again."

Madeleine squeaked with mock-terror and peered up.

"Well wasn't Cuddy an old Chauvinist pig? What do you say to that, Bertrand?"

Bertrand paced back and forth, scanning the ceiling.

"I would say it was more superstitious poppycock. I can see no evidence of repair to the vaulting. And falling masonry would inevitably have scarred this marble slab, which you can see is perfectly smooth and polished."

Madeleine smiled at him in a way Beth loathed.

"Getting rattled, dear? Poor old Bertrand. If you can't touch something with your hand, or smell it or measure it, it doesn't exist for you, darling. Does it? So *you* won't mind me putting my foot on old Cuddy, will you? It won't mean a thing – except Woman's Lib forever!"

The old man drew back. Bertrand said, "Don't make a fool of yourself, Madeleine."

Beth stared in horror. There was a real saint down there. Father Wilson preached about him. *Please*, Madeleine, she thought desperately, please don't meddle with things you don't understand.

Then Madeleine saw Beth's face.

"Oh, I'm shocking our little Christian here. *So* unlike her beloved father. Don't be such a prig, Beth. It doesn't mean a thing." And she placed her blue shoe on the black marble slab.

Nothing moved; nothing fell. But in that instant Beth knew that someone had become aware of them.

III

Perhaps it was only the cathedral verger. Perhaps he'd been watching them for some time. Now he stepped forward and asked them in a sharp voice to leave the cathedral. They left quickly and ashamed, like children.

Outside, Madeleine wailed, "I haven't bought any picture-postcards. I *wanted* some picture-postcards!"

"Go back and get some then," said Bertrand. "We'll wait here."

"Oh, I can't be bothered," said Madeleine, though she usually liked keeping people waiting.

Back in the Volvo, Beth could hear her father taking deep breaths to calm himself. He always said you made mistakes when you were angry, and no one could afford to make mistakes driving. But deep breaths or not, they took the wrong turning out of town, and didn't discover their mistake till Brancepeth. Then they got lost coming out of the Tyne Tunnel and only covered twenty miles in two hours. They lost contact with Madeleine and when she finally found them, all the stuffing had been knocked out of her. She tamely followed the Volvo.

The three children, having refused to ride with her, stared at her stonily out of the rear window, or ignored her. She drove with her chin up, pretending she didn't care.

Perhaps they were all tired. The Great North Road rolled endlessly, and the warmth had gone out of the late August sun.

"I'm cold," said Sally. "Someone's walking over my grave."

Bertrand frowned, but he turned on the heater and the radio. The music was comforting.

"I know what Sally means," said Michael. "The sky's so lonely and big in Northumberland."

"The sky's the normal size," said Bertrand. "It's just lack of tall buildings and trees."

"There are trees, but they're losing their leaves already. And they're so little, and all their branches bend to the left."

"Prevailing wind," said Bertrand. "North-east gales. The wind comes straight from Norway; you need two sweaters here, even in summer."

"You feel the soil's so thin," said Beth. "The rocks are like bones sticking through skin."

"Cambridge has made you lot soft," said Bertrand firmly. "This place will harden you up."

"You mean harden up our skins like a rhinoceros?" said Sally. "Then we shan't be able to sit down."

It was good to laugh.

"Will there be a lady to look after us, where we're going? Like Mrs Madden?" asked Sally.

"No – stupid," said Michael. "We're looking after ourselves this trip. This is your daddy's house – he owns it."

"Our house is in Cambridge!"

"Not *that* one, dope. This is the one Uncle Henry left to your daddy in his will."

"Will Uncle Henry be there?"

"No, dope. People don't leave people houses in their wills till they're *dead*."

"Is Uncle Henry dead, Daddy?"

"Yes. And stop calling her a stupid dope, Michael. She might end up believing you. Shall I tell you about wills, Sally?"

"Yes, Daddy." But she wasn't listening. She was staring at the bleak lines of the approaching hills, sucking the thumb of her bad hand. Beth saw her father's mouth tighten. He said sharply, "Stop being a baby, Sally!"

The thumb was removed, but crept slowly back. To

distract her father, Beth said, "What was Uncle Henry *like*, Daddy?"

"I hardly knew him. He was a brilliant man in his younger days – Fellow of my college. Had me to dinner in his rooms my first term up. Just come back from Arabia – he knocked around the world a lot then. He said he'd caught a mermaid, Sally … Sally, are you listening?"

"Sally," yelled Beth, "Daddy's just said Uncle Henry caught a mermaid."

"Mmmm," said Sally, thumb in mouth. "Perhaps *she* looked after the house. Perhaps she'll be there to look after us, like Mrs Madden."

"Be better than Madeleine's toad-in-the-hole," said Michael. "And baked beans on toast four times a week."

"As I was saying," said Bertrand firmly, "I never got the chance to know Uncle Henry. He was in the middle of a most promising career when he inherited this house. He just resigned everything and went to live in it, and no one ever saw him again. Nobody that *mattered* anyway. As I told you, I'd forgotten he existed till the lawyer wrote to me about the will."

"Are you sure the house will be all right to live in?" said Beth dubiously, for about the tenth time.

"That remains to be seen. The lawyer said it was fit to live in. Nothing's been changed since Henry died, and he lived there."

"Did he die there?" asked Sally.

"No. He was drowned at sea."

"Oh."

"He was very old – over seventy. Everyone has to die sometime."

"Yes." Sally went back to her thumb, and Beth to her worrying.

"I keep wondering what it will be like," she said at last.

"Pretty big, pretty old and pretty far from anywhere, I

should think," said her father. "More or less on the beach. We've to take the lane to Budle Point."

Silence fell.

"Looking forward to the sailing dinghy?" asked Bertrand.

That cheered Beth up. In fact she had to stop herself from gloating. The family had sailed a lot, till Madeleine came. Bertrand had tried to teach Madeleine. But after ten minutes Madeleine had pronounced sailing stupid and they hadn't sailed since. If there was sailing they'd be all together again – a tight little family with Mike but without Madeleine.

Yet still Beth worried.

"Will there be everything there for us? I mean there won't be shops …"

"We'll have to stock up in Alnwick, assuming we get there before closing. The lawyer said there were sheets and blankets, pots and pans. Calor gas; no electricity or anything like that and the loo's a chemical thing, but we'll manage. It's not the Arctic, you know."

He looked at her, a little worried and guilty. She forced a smile; he squeezed her hand.

"We'll manage, you and I."

The squeeze made everything all right.

Alnwick was a scramble. Bertrand hurried to the lawyer's to pick up the keys. All the shops were shut, but Madeleine managed to re-open the biggest grocer's by smiling and grimacing at the owner through the window.

She hadn't made a shopping list. She simply bought too much of everything to make sure she had enough. She kept thinking of one more thing. She gave the grocer a lecture on French butter. She ordered three dozen large eggs, changed her mind and ordered medium, and then went back to large again. The grocer's wife went off into a corner, glaring and muttering, looking at her watch and switching off the lights. But the large bald grocer seemed entranced. The more

Madeleine messed him about, the more he smiled. He ended up carrying a mountain of groceries out to the Volvo, bowing and scraping like something out of "Upstairs, Downstairs". When he finally went back into his shop he and his wife began to have a row.

Bertrand reappeared, with a bundle of large keys and an electric lantern; the kind you see at road accidents.

"Dinner," he said, "and it's going to be a good one. Can't beat plunging into the unknown on a full stomach." He said it as a joke; no one laughed.

Madeleine opened her mouth, but Bertrand held up a hand.

"No more snack-bars. I've booked at the White Swan."

The Swan was old but cosy, with white tablecloths, good fire and friendly waiter. As he took the order, Madeleine turned on the charm.

"This is much nicer than I expected. You've got such an awful front window … those cobwebs …

The waiter grinned.

"You mean the dirty bottles, madam? Wey, them's famous the world over. The locals call this place the 'Dirty Bottles' not the 'White Swan'. Don't you knaa the story behind it?"

"*Do* tell us!"

"Wey, aboot two hundred year ago, the landlord was putting them bottles in that window – for display, like. They was all new and shiny in those days, o' course. Anyway, he dropped doon dead of a heart attack. After he was buried, no one felt like moving them bottles much – superstition, aah suppose. Anyways, this smart city slicker comes along – a southerner aah believe – 'Aah'll move them bottles,' he says. So he moves the first one, and drops doon dead too. They haven't been moved since."

Madeleine's eyes shone.

"*Really*? Could I just take a *peep*?"

"Well, I don't know …" said the waiter, doubtfully.

"I do," said Bertrand quietly. "Madeleine, you will not go near those bottles, if I have to put a judo hold on you. Is that quite clear?"

Beth suddenly realised what her father looked like, with his beaky nose, large eyes and tawny hair. A kestrel. Kestrels looked gentler than the bigger hawks, but they still killed other birds. She had never thought of her father like this before.

Bertrand turned to the waiter.

"I have been listening to superstitious rubbish all day. The further you get from London, the worse it gets. I suppose you have a local headless horseman?"

The waiter flinched at the sarcasm.

"No, sir."

"Any white ladies, black dogs, phantom coachmen?"

"No, sir."

"Perhaps Merlin's buried near here? Or King Arthur and his knights?"

"No, sir."

"Then kindly fetch our meal."

"Yes, sir." He went scurrying.

Madeleine looked up with a last spurt of spirit.

"Bertrand, did anyone ever tell you what a bastard you are?"

"You did, dear, often."

Madeleine dropped her eyes to the table like a chastised child. For once, Beth found herself sympathising.

"Two miles to go," said Beth, reading the map. "Turn right, down a little lane past the castle."

She wished it would get properly dark. But the sunlight just withered and withered, like an old painting. To the right, sand-dunes flicked past endlessly, each looking the same as the last. Beyond the dunes was a line of surf, and beyond that a bank of mist, fifty yards out to sea. Wave after wave appeared out of nowhere; like ghosts. In the mist a bell was tolling. The mist reached out fingers across the road. Sea air came in through the open car-window, making the back of your hands damp.

"There's *another* headless horseman!" shouted Michael. Sally gave a mock-scream and giggled. She was snuggled up to Michael.

"How many headless horsemen is that, Sally?"

"Eighteen, Michael." She giggled again; she was happy. How was she to know that Michael was getting his revenge on Bertrand for the scene in the restaurant?

Beth sighed. Both the joke and Bertrand's temper were wearing thin.

They passed a great blur in the mist.

"What was *that*, Michael?"

"That was a headless castle, Sally. Where all the headless horsemen live. There were three on the battlements, darning their socks."

"There's the lane, Daddy," said Beth.

Now they were among the dunes. Sand spilled across the lane, making the car lurch. Then the sun went down suddenly, like a lamp extinguished. Bertrand switched on his lights; the lights of the Spitfire came on behind. As if in answer, ahead, a lighthouse came on, revolving, blinking.

"Oh, look," said Sally. And dimly they saw Budle Point, a great shield of black stone, curving into the sea. On top of the shield, a few shabby holiday cottages swam past in the gloom. There were no lights in their windows. They made the place seem lonelier.

The road dipped, and a pair of low roofs came into view, down by the beach. Bertrand put on the hand-brake, switched off the engine, and they sat listening to the noise of the sea and the bell.

"Hey, look," said Michael. "Lighthouses out to sea. That mist's gone. Like magic!"

"It was heat-haze," said Bertrand. "It goes when the sun goes down. Those lighthouses are on the Farne Islands, Michael. One on the Longstone, and one on Inner Farne."

"Oho, we've got nice neighbours, then."

"Who's that?" said Bertrand sharply.

"Cuddy lived on Inner Farne," said Michael, and laughed. His laugh was just like Madeleine's.

IV

"Everyone carry something; it'll save a journey," said Bertrand. They struggled down through the sand, laden with suitcases. Even Sally carried the transistor radio with her good hand.

The sand had gained since Uncle Henry died, creeping off the dunes and breaking the garden fence, smothering the salt-bitten roses and banking itself a foot deep against the front door.

Bertrand tried the big keys one after another. Each grated rustily in the lock, but none turned.

"He's given me the wrong keys. Here, shine the torch, Beth." Beth shone the torch. The keys were huge, like church keys, tied together with a big piece of cardboard on which someone had scrawled *Monk's Heugh* in biro.

"Is this Monk's Heugh?"

"So it would seem," said her father. She could tell he didn't like the name. Was that why he hadn't told them about it? "Perhaps the lock's rusted solid."

Michael reached forward and rattled the door-handle in frustration.

"Don't be an ass, Michael. That won't open it."

But it did. The smell of wallpaper and mice came out.

"Unlocked," said Madeleine. "How awful – how irresponsible – anyone could have got in – three months standing empty."

"I don't think folk lock their doors much round here," said Bertrand stiffly.

"That's not the point – you don't know what – uurgh," said Madeleine pressing home her small victory.

"I'll see that lawyer in the morning."

"Locking the stable door after the horse has bolted."

*

Beth lay on her back, rubbing her feet together to get them warm. In her mind's eye, she roamed the corridors of the old house lying silent round her. Such long corridors, twisting left and right, up and down, for no reason. So many rooms, with strips of damp wallpaper moving in the breeze from windows that wouldn't shut.

How many rooms? A sitting-room each side of the front door. A dining-room each side behind that. No – they had decided the one on the right must have been Uncle Henry's study.

Then a door they couldn't unlock on the left, and the kitchen on the right. Then a scullery bigger than the kitchen, then a pantry nearly as big. As for upstairs … her mind gave up. The low grey house with its grey stone roof went on forever.

"Beth?" Sally's voice, from the other bed, sounded quavery.

"Yes?"

"Can I sleep in your bed tonight?"

Beth considered. Her father didn't like girls sharing a bed. But the sheets were damp and her hot-water bottle had long since lost its heat. Two sleep warmer than one; if anyone *could* sleep after the last three hours.

"O.K. then."

Sally snuggled in like a little animal. Then she squeaked as light showed all round the edge of the bedroom door. Someone knocked.

"Who is it?"

"Mike. Can I come in?"

"O.K." Mike was a sight. He had his dressing-gown pulled over his head like a monk's hood, and two blankets wrapped round his legs.

22

"God, it's bloody freezing. Can I sit on your bed? I've got some chocolate."

"But we've cleaned our teeth. Bertrand says …"

"Stuff Bertrand – he brought us here. What does he want us to do, die of exposure? My hot-water bottle's useless."

"We couldn't get the kettle to boil. The gas-cylinder gave out and the wood for the fire was damp."

"This is a right bloody hole if you ask me. Uncle Henry must have been bonkers. D'you know what I've got in my room? A photo of a lifeboat-crew, with dribbles of moisture running down it. They all drowned in the Great Storm of 1873."

"And these glass cases everywhere. Stuffed seagulls and dried flying-fish."

"*And* there's a human skull with a bullet-hole straight through it. Trawled up by a fishing-boat off Craster Point in 1902."

"Eeurk!" said Sally.

"What do you think Uncle Henry was? He's got everything beautifully labelled."

"A nut, girl. A fully-licensed Cambridge nut. It gets some of them that way, my mother says. She reckons Bertrand will go that way in the end."

"Oh shut up. Your mother's a fool."

"Yeah, but she has her uses. *She* found the paraffin and got the fire going with it."

"She nearly burnt the house down."

"Pity she didn't. Then we could all go back to the White Swan at Alnwick."

They munched chocolate in mild contentment, slowly moving closer together and feeling warmer. It was quite bearable now there were three.

"There's a dead creepy pong in this room," said Mike in an mock-ominous voice.

"Oh, shut up," said Beth. "*You* haven't got to sleep here."

"There *is* a pong," said Sally. "It's from some more funny things, under the bed. In a tashy case."

"What *kind* of things?" said Beth sharply.

"Dunno. *Funny* things. Show you."

Mike shone his torch, and Sally pulled out an attaché case of ancient curling leather, with brass locks. On the side of the case was stamped *H.S.*.

"Henry Studdard."

"D'you think Uncle Henry slept in this bed?" asked Sally.

"Open the case," said Beth. Sally clicked open the brass locks one by one, tongue curling out of the corner of her mouth with the effort.

"*What* a pong," said Mike. "Smells like a rugby changing-room."

"What *are* they?" whispered Beth.

"Boots," said Mike, picking one up. "Number nines. They're black with grease – on the inside! Someone hasn't been changing their socks …"

"But they're so crude – no proper soles and heels, and nasty big stitching. And the left one's the same as the right. They'd *cripple* you if you tried to wear them."

"Bit like the Cavaliers wore in the Civil War – no left or right fitting. Why d'you think they rode horses? They didn't dare walk."

"Oh, they're older than Cavaliers' boots. Much cruder."

"Oh, yes, Clever Dick? Well someone's been wearing them recently. A pong like that doesn't last hundreds of years."

"Perhaps some old tramp?"

"No self-respecting tramp would touch them."

"What's the other thing?" asked Sally.

Mike picked it up. It was the shape of a deflated football.

"Eeergh! It's all damp and mouldy."

"What *is* it?"

Mike dug his fingers in, and crumbled a piece off. The sharp smell of mould came to their nostrils.

"It's bread! Fancy a slice with butter? Solider than a school-dinner pudding. One hit with this would have sunk the Bismarck. Someone was a lousy cook."

"What's that mark on it?"

Mike held his torch at an angle, and a large cross stood out in shadow on top of the loaf.

"Hot cross bun," said Mike. "And don't try telling me that *this* is medieval. It's not more than six months old. Any older and the mould would've destroyed it. *That's* 'O' level biology."

"What's this?" said Sally, holding up a piece of paper. Beth brought it close to the torch.

"Uncle Henry's writing."

"It *would* be. Now tell us some news."

Beth read, "*At last I have proof. Loaf from the hospitium. They made him take off the boots, and threw them over the cliff. Then they washed his feet and gave him a new pair. 8th February 1976.*"

"Wasn't that just before Henry died?" she asked.

There was a long silence. Then Mike said, "So what? We know what Uncle Henry was like – look at all the weird things he's collected here. Some castaway boots off some old tramp would be right up his alley."

"But who are the 'they' who threw the boots over the cliff?"

"The Welfare people, stupid. Do-gooders."

"Throwing boots over a *cliff*? And that word *hospitium*. It means guest-room. The only place they had them was in monasteries. And the bread. Henry *must* have thought these things important."

"Oh, Jeepers," said Mike in exasperation. "You could waste the rest of your life working out what old Henry got up to. Old people are crazy. I had a great-uncle used to make models of Tower Bridge with hundreds of lollipop-sticks."

"But there was a cross on the loaf …"

Mike climbed back on the bed. "If you want my advice, slat the whole thing over the cliff in the morning, before you catch something fatal off it. Anybody want more chocolate?"

Beth put the things back in the case, snapped the locks shut and pushed it under the bed again.

"Michael?" said Sally. "Can I borrow your torch?"

"O.K. But don't waste the battery. Haven't got a spare."

The torch-beam swung round the room, lancing into the deeper shadows where the bedtime candle hadn't reached. It was quite good fun, because there were three together.

Then the torch lanced into the shadow above the huge wardrobe.

A hollow-eyed face peered down at them.

V

Sally really screamed this time; enough to waken the dead. She burrowed under the sheets. The torch went rolling across the bed and fell on the floor. It didn't break but went on rolling, ending up a little pool of light in the corner. But it still cast a faint glow on the rest of the room, and Beth could see the face on the wardrobe glimmering faintly. She knew she could only move if the thing came to get Sally. Only that would give her enough animal courage.

"Silly ass," said Michael quite cheerfully. He got off the bed and retrieved the torch. Had he *no* fear? He shone the torch full into the shadow above the wardrobe. The hollow face reappeared, and shoulders and a body. It was quite still.

"Silly ass," said Michael again, walking towards it. A square of shining light appeared in front of the face, almost hiding it. Michael put a chair against the wardrobe, and climbed up to the face.

"Silly ass – it's only more of Uncle Henry's collection. It's inside a glass case. I think it's Henry's mermaid." He rapped on the glass and said, "Hallo, Sailor," to the mermaid in his mocking-voice.

At that moment the bedroom door burst open with a flood of light.

"What the devil's going on?" demanded Bertrand. He didn't look impressive. His dressing-gown collar was inside-out and his hair stood upright in a ginger fuzz. By contrast, Madeleine was looking glamorous in something with a fur collar; she even appeared to have combed her hair.

"Hallo, Sailor," screeched Michael again, from the wardrobe top, making them jump, and then laughing maliciously. "I'm just chatting-up Henry's mermaid."

"Heavens, it *is* a mermaid!" said Madeleine with delight, and joined her son. "What do you say to that, Bertrand? I thought mermaids didn't exist?"

"Don't be silly – it's a dugong – a seagoing mammal like a seal. See, it's got whiskers, and flippers – *not* a fish's tail. The dugong started the mermaid myth. Every stuffed mermaid the old sailors fetched home was really a dugong – or some jiggery-pokery with a stuffed monkey for a top, and a stuffed fish for a tail."

"Thanks for the lecture," said Madeleine. "Spoilsport!"

Beth got out of bed on shaking legs; but as she got close to the glass case her fear turned to pity. The dugong was falling apart, its skin splitting and flaking like old paint, its once-full breasts mere flaps of skin. It reminded her of a broken mechanical monkey she'd once seen at a fairground. Yet it was not mechanical; once it had been alive.

"Poor thing!"

"Poor thing!" echoed Sally, peering out of the bedclothes, red-faced and near-suffocated.

"What are you doing in *Beth's* bed?" said Bertrand ominously. He always got angry after a fright. "And what's Michael doing here at all?"

"I heard the scream and came to help," lied Michael, with superb righteous indignation.

"You were *very* quick," said Bertrand. "And that doesn't explain what Sally's doing in Beth's bed."

Beth was silent. She'd never lied to her father. But if she didn't lie now, she would let down Michael. And once Bertrand found what was going on, there would be no more comfort of three together, when night closed down on this ghastly place. Everyone would have to stay in their own room and bed; neat, tidy and miserable. So she lied.

"Sally screamed and ran to me; she was having a nightmare." Her father gave her a hard look, and she could feel herself blushing. Bertrand looked at Sally. Sally lied too, with a silent nod. Then she reached down among the bedclothes and put something in her mouth for comfort.

"Chocolate," said Bertrand, in a voice like thunder. "Chocolate after you've cleaned your teeth."

"It's *my* chocolate," said Michael. "I was eating it when Sally screamed. I must have brought it with me."

"You know the rules."

"I've always eaten chocolate in bed … before …" He stopped, but everyone knew he meant "before you married my mother".

Madeleine leapt to her son's rescue.

"Oh, come *on*, Bertrand. I'm frozen. There's nothing that can't wait till morning." Bertrand huffed and puffed. Sally was sent back to shiver in her own bed. Michael sidled off down the corridor with a last defiant "Hallo, Sailor". Madeleine said crossly, "Oh, for God's sake," and swept off in a flurry of fur. Beth and Bertrand were left staring at each other.

"I want the truth, Beth."

Suddenly her father did not seem so wonderful. She rather preferred Michael's lying gallantry; and the way his mother backed him up. Madeleine understood that people sometimes needed to break the rules, because she broke rules herself.

So Beth put up a hand to shade her eyes and said coldly, "Please turn that lantern away – you're blinding me."

"I find this regrettable," said Bertrand stiffly. "Goodnight."

The darkness returned, in which the dugong waited, its skin forever cracking and peeling … darkness with the smell of salt and the sound of the sea.

"Beth," said a very small voice. "Beth, can I come back in your bed? I'm so cold."

She snuggled in, and Beth was glad she was there.

VI

It was better in the morning. The sun shone. There was a roaring fire in the kitchen stove, and the smell of bacon and eggs.

But Sally was still sucking the thumb of her bad hand.

"I was frightened of the mermaid."

"And I'm not surprised," said Madeleine, with her usual extravagant sympathy. "This place is enough to frighten anybody. It's like living in a museum of the *nastiest* kind. Do you know what I found in the bread-bin this morning? Human vertebrae! Your uncle must have been *mad*." She tossed three blackened lumps on the tablecloth, tied together with a label.

Bertrand picked them up curiously and read the label. "Henry found them in a peat-bog. They could be prehistoric. Notice how dark they are? Peat-bogs preserve things marvellously."

"Well they can be preserved elsewhere. I'm having a springclean this morning and the whole lot's going out to the dustbin."

Bertrand stared aghast; he swallowed several times before he was able to speak.

"You can't do that. This is a scientific collection, made by a scholar. Henry spent thirty years on it … you could destroy something irreplaceable. I've got to have time to examine it … contact Newcastle Museum …"

"If you think I'm going to spend one more night in this unspeakable human junkshop –"

"Now *listen*. I'm going to Alnwick to hire the sailing dinghy this morning. We'd better give her a trial sail this afternoon. I'll start looking at Henry's stuff this evening."

"You'll find it by the dustbin, then!"

The children drifted un-noticed out of the room, and onto the windy freedom of the dunes. Michael looked at Beth with a grin.

"This row's going to be a gale-force effort. How long shall we give them?"

He made Beth laugh in spite of herself.

"Two hours, I think."

But it wasn't really funny.

"Loosen the main-sheet," said Bertrand, "and slacken the jib a little. And you're steering too far to port. You'll have us in irons in a minute."

"I've only got two hands," yelled Mike.

"Try to be patient," said Bertrand, with utterly maddening reasonableness. "Rome wasn't built in a day."

"Stuff Rome," muttered Mike under his breath, but loud enough for Bertrand to hear. "I wish we'd hired a motorboat."

After an hour of Bertrand's sailing-tuition, Mike had lost all his ideas about the romance of sail. Bertrand made you do the same thing over and over again, till you were perfect. It was worse than a school geometry lesson.

But there were compensations. The sun winked on the blue water; everything smelt as clean as new washing; and there were the marvellous Farne Islands.

Except, as usual, Bertrand knew everything about them.

"Har-car, Har-car!" chanted Sally. "What a funny name."

"It's a Viking name. The Vikings gave all these islands their names. Nothing's changed much round here since Viking times."

"Glororum Shad's not a Viking name," said Mike. "Sounds more Latin."

Bertrand considered, head on one side like a bird.

"Ah, yes. One might say that Glororum Shad's the exception

that proves the rule. There's a village on the mainland called Glororum – something to do with the monks who lived on Holy Island, I presume. So shall we say nothing much has changed since the Viking's *and* monk's time?"

He smiled at Michael tolerantly.

Is he *human*? thought Michael, and said viciously, "Bet the Vikings thumped hell out of the monks."

Bertrand winced at such crudeness; then controlled himself and said, "Yes, the Vikings burnt Holy Island monastery twice; in A.D. 793 and again in 875."

"Murderous bastards," said Mike appreciatively.

"That's a rather imprecise way of seeing it," said Bertrand coldly. "There was certainly a conflict of cultures, but it's too easy to condemn the Vikings as mere villains. They were, after all, obeying their own ethical code. Doing their own thing, as you would say. They were superb navigators, discovered America five hundred years before Columbus, and their wood-carving is magnificent. They weren't just thugs."

"Bet old Cuddy wouldn't have agreed with you," said Mike. "Not when he saw them burning *his* monastery."

Beth saw her father go pale with rage and changed the subject quickly.

"What's that white streak on Inner Farne – it looks like a vein of white marble …" Her voice went romantic and dreamy.

"Bird-shit!" said Mike viciously.

"Actually, it's waste carbide from the lighthouse," said Bertrand. "The keepers have thrown it down the cliff-face for years."

God, thought Mike, it's like living with the Encyclopaedia Brittanica.

Sally saved the day.

"Glorororororum! Glorororororororororom! Glorororororum!"

When Sally started that caper, everyone ducked for cover.

Once started she could go on for hours.

They went on sailing round the islands. Finally Mike said, "Why do we keep going round the edge? Why can't we go and land on the islands? Might find a wreck or something!"

"Two reasons," said Bertrand. "First, the islands are a bird-sanctuary. You need a permit to land.

"Second, there are reefs just under water. It's no place for fools. Only the local fishermen know it well, and they only go in motor-boats. In a sailing-dinghy the islands would rob you of the wind, you'd get caught in a strong current, and then *you'd* be the wreck … especially people who can't tell port from starboard."

"Oh, thanks for the lecture, professor. Who do you think you are? Mr Green Cross Code? You spend all your time thinking up good reasons why nobody can do anything interesting at all!"

"Pull in your mainsail – you're losing the wind," snapped Bertrand. "And *look* where you're *sailing*."

Michael leapt to his feet, making the dinghy rock wildly.

"Stuff your rotten boat. If you're so clever, *you* sail her."

He went and sat by the mast with his back to them all.

"Aren't there motor-boats that take you out to the Farnes, Daddy?" said Beth, trying to be helpful.

"Every day, from Seahouses. Visitors are allowed to land on Inner Farne and Brownsman."

"You see, Michael, there's always a way." She touched his shoulder sympathetically. Mike shook her hand off.

"Leave him," said Bertrand. "He'll get over it."

But he didn't. They sat in miserable silence all the way home. Except for Sally saying "Glororororum".

VII

They helped Bertrand beach the boat.

"You three go ahead," he said. "This dinghy needs a bit of attention. The rudder-pintle's stiff, and one of the stays needs replacing. I may have to go into Alnwick again."

Mike and Beth let Sally go glororuming ahead. Mike said bitterly, "Does your father always have to have *everything* exactly right? How can you bear to live with him?"

Beth sat down on a tuft of spear-grass.

"Don't be unfair, Mike. In his job, if you aren't *exactly* right, other people make a fool of you. Dons can be awfully cruel, you know."

"Oh, I can see that. But does he have to bring it home with him?"

"He found it hard after my mother died. It's not easy bringing up two daughters alone, you know."

"Madeleine had a rough time after my father died. But she muddled through without dotting every 'i' and crossing every 't'."

Beth bit back a catty remark just in time. Instead she said, "Don't brood. Perhaps we can go to Seahouses tomorrow, and get a boat to the Farnes."

Michael laughed suddenly.

"I can't fight with you, Beth, can I?"

"No."

"You're a funny girl. Always wanting other people to be happy. But what makes *you* happy, Beth?"

She thought a long time, biting her lip on one side.

"I don't know. Other people being happy, I suppose. Things being *right*."

"You're too good for this world. Don't you want anything

34

for *you*? You should be a bloody nun."

She said, quietly, "I've sometimes thought of becoming a nun."

A dozen jokes about nuns swept through Mike's head. But he managed to keep his mouth shut, which truly amazed him. He only said, "Bertrand wouldn't dig that much. Him being an atheist and all."

Beth said, "That's one of the things that would stop me; that I might only want to be a nun to … spite Bertrand. But he wouldn't stop me, you know. He wants people to be free."

"Except being free to wreck boats and drown themselves."

She laughed and punched him. "Come on, you've tried that line once already."

As they stood up, Sally came running back.

"Madeleine's gone out," she said, looking worried, "and that mermaid's in the yard."

There was a note pinned to the front door.

Gone to Newcastle. Expect me when you see me. Don't touch the RUBBISH! Madeleine.

The rubbish lay by the dustbin. It was mainly bones and framed photographs. The skull with the bullet-hole lay grinning on top. The biggest item was the dugong in its glass case. Heaven knows how Madeleine had managed to lift it. But she'd cracked the glass lid in the process, and a piece of glass lay inside.

"Jee-hoshaphat!" Mike whistled. "*Now* there's going to be a row. Expect she got in a panic when she broke the glass, and that's why she's scarpered off to Newcastle."

Waves of dread flowed over Beth as she thought of the scene to come; Bertrand and Madeleine mightn't be on speaking terms for the rest of the holiday.

But beyond that, there was her odd pity for the dugong.

Some violent movement of Madeleine's had thrown it on one side. The place where it sat on its artificial rock had torn, and stuffing was trickling out. And a few drops of rain fell as she watched, making a pinging noise on the glass top of the case. If it wasn't rescued soon, the dugong would be merely a heap of fragments. And it had once been a living thing, free in the sea.

"Can't we find a safe place for it?"

"Put it back in the house, and Madeleine will knock your head off."

Beth wrung her hands.

"Oh … oh … oh." She was suddenly and absurdly close to tears.

"Hey, steady on," said Mike. "Let me think. Uncle Mike's the boy to have ideas. What about *that*?"

He pointed along the dunes. There was a black tarred hut fifty yards away, quite by itself, nearer the sea than the house. They'd noticed it before, without bothering.

"But it *belongs* to somebody."

"Like who? How do you know it doesn't belong with this house?"

"How can we tell?"

"Easy," said Mike reaching behind the front door. "We'll try these keys. If one fits, it belongs to us."

They walked to the hut. Close-to, it was surprisingly large. And the last key Mike tried fitted the lock.

"It's always the last key you try," said Mike.

"Of course," said Beth, feeling much happier. Together they swung back the double-doors, but they stuck halfway in the sand.

"Doesn't it pong?" said Sally, holding her nose.

"Bet there's a pirate's skeleton," roared Mike, leaping about on one leg like Long John Silver. "Aha, Jim lad!" Sally gave a delighted scream.

But there were no skeletons. Mike crashed about inside,

and threw out several great strong baskets, bleached pale grey.

"Lobster-pots!" Then he emerged draped in yards of black fishing-net, with cork-floats attached, pretending to be a ghost.

"Stop messing, Mike," said Beth. "It's *really* going to rain soon."

"Go and get the torch," said Mike. "It's as black as the hobs of hell in here, and packed solid. We'll have to move stuff about to make room."

When Beth returned, Mike had forced the double-doors back, and a lot of fishing-gear lay on the sand. Mike emerged, holding a long pole with a cork float and flag on top, pretending to be a Bengal Lancer.

"That's only a marker-buoy," said Beth crossly. "Let me get inside and have a look."

"There's something big in there – *really* big. Made of wood. Everything's piled up so much around it, I can't see what it is."

The thing was made of black curved planks. They worked feverishly to clear it.

"Hey," said Mike suddenly, in awed tones. "It's a boat! A *real* boat, not a fibreglass thing. If we can fix it, we can ..."

In her mind, Beth finished the sentence for him: ... *we can sail off to the Farnes without Bertrand being there, stopping us having fun.* Oh, Mike, you incredible optimist! How little you know my father.

"It's like a Viking's ship," announced Sally, breathless. They stared. It *was* like a Viking-ship, only smaller: the same high graceful bow sweeping away in low smooth curves.

A voice spoke from behind.

"Of course it's like a Viking-ship. Haven't you noticed? All the fishing-cobles round here are like Viking-ships. The design has come down from their day to this."

Bertrand was peering over their shoulders, with the greatest possible interest.

"Ah," said Mike, "the local fishing-cobles have *fronts* like Viking-ships. But they've got flat sterns. This one's got a stern like a Viking-ship too."

"Quite right," said Bertrand, refusing to be drawn into another squabble. "How very observant of you, Mike. This is a highly-interesting variation. I've never seen one like it before. I wonder if one could trace the origin. Let me see. Saunders does Maritime History. He might be able to …"

VIII

All four of them worked like mad until the boat had been cleared, and hauled out onto the beach. Bertrand was so excited that he helped stow away the dugong in the shed without a murmur. And the photographs and bones. He only had eyes for the new discovery. He prowled back and forth like a detective on a new case, or a dog with a new bone.

"It's exceedingly primitive," he said. "Notice how the rowlocks are carved out of the wood of the boat, instead of being separate brass fittings. That means it's definitely pre-Victorian."

"The boats on the lake at home have got rowlocks like that," objected Mike. But Beth kicked him on the ankle, and Bertrand didn't even hear him, as he swept on.

"It's been used for sailing – but the mountings for the rigging are just holes bored in the sides. Bedrock design, you might say. Crude and clumsy, but perfectly effective."

"Can we sail her?" asked Mike.

"Heavens, no. Her timbers must be quite rotten." Bertrand took out a sailor's knife with a spike and drove it into the timbers.

"Ouch." The knife sprang from his hand, leaving not a dent.

"Why, it's as hard as iron. Must be oak."

"Rotten, eh?" asked Mike and began to sing. "*Heart of oak are our ships ...*"

"Shut up, ass," said Beth. "How old is it, Daddy?"

"Impossible to say. It's carrying a dozen coats of pitch. But it's been repaired and repaired. Just look where the ropes have worn these bits smooth."

"Bet she'd sail jolly fast," said Mike hopefully. Then he wished he hadn't, because that sent Bertrand off into another lecture.

"These cobles weren't built for speed like a modern dinghy. They're built to ride the waves in all weathers, so the fisherman can stand up and use both hands to get in lobster-pots, without being pitched overboard by a fluke wave. Oh, she'll be a grand sea-boat, but don't expect speed out of her. She's too round and broad in the beam."

"She does look rather like a pregnant duck," said Mike grinning at Beth.

"She's beautiful," wailed Beth. "How can you say a thing like that?"

"And she's got a *name*," said Sally, as if that made any difference.

"What – the *Dirty Duck*?"

"No, Michael!" Sally stamped her foot. "But I can't read it quite. What does it say, Daddy?"

Bertrand crouched behind his younger daughter; they all peered at the bow. There were certainly marks under the pitch which *could* have been carved lettering. On the other hand, as Mike pointed out, they could have been dents caused by bumping into stone jetties.

"It *is* letters," said Beth, tracing the marks with her finger. "That's an *R*. And then something else, and then an *S. Rosur* or *Rasor*."

"Whoever heard of a ship called the *Razor*?" jeered Mike. "Built by Gillette or Wilkinson Sword? From the hands of the finest craftsmen ... boom, boom-boom." He did his too-well-known impersonation of the television advert.

But Bertrand stood frowning. "It's very old lettering. I think you're right, Beth. *R* ... that looks like an *E* ... *S*, yes ... *U*, *R* and another *R* and another *E*. If it's a ship's name it's an incredibly long one, though. Look, it goes right round to here ... *S*, *U*, *M*."

"The middle of the name's been scraped right away," said Beth. "It must have been in some collision."

"It doesn't have to be all one name," said Mike. "Ships carry their port of origin too – like *Queen Elizabeth II Southampton*."

"But what port ends with *sum*?" said Beth.

They looked at each other blankly.

"There's a river in East Anglia called the Wensum," said Bertrand. (Trust *him* to know.) "It might have a port at the mouth of it, I suppose. But I never *heard* of it."

"Then it can't *possibly* exist," said Michael. He raised his voice to a high queenly squeak.

"I christen this ship *Resurre of Sum*. May God bless her, and may all who sail in her get their *sums* wrong."

Everybody groaned.

"Could you make her sail?" asked Beth.

Bertrand sounded doubtful. "She's big, you know – must be nearly a twenty-footer. And she's heavy. But she'd have certain advantages. We could all go fishing in her; even Madeleine might come."

"Who's taking my name in vain?" said a sharp voice. "And what the hell is *that*? More of Henry's mucky rubbish?"

She was standing behind them, hands on the hips of her yellow trousers. Her sharp eyes hadn't missed the dugong, now safely in its shed; *or* the fact that everyone was enjoying themselves, either. She looked cheated.

"You'll not get me in that thing. Anyway, you couldn't get it to sail, Bertrand. Even an expert couldn't."

Beth watched her father set his jaw grimly; Madeleine's sarcasm had achieved what the children's pleading might never have done. *Resurre of Sum* would sail now, if Bertrand killed himself in the attempt.

"We shall need an eighteen-foot aluminium-alloy mast ... and ..."

"I suppose nobody's bothered to cook any tea," said

41

Madeleine nastily. But everyone just looked at her and she stamped off indoors, deprived of her quarrel.

IX

Next afternoon, Expedition Farne lay on the cliffs of its destination in curiously happy mood; mainly because, though it had started five-strong, it was now reduced to two.

"Peaceful, innit?" said Mike, kicking his legs.

"Lovely," said Beth, peering down into the calm green water.

"I'm glad the others didn't come."

Beth tried to look shocked, and then giggled.

"That cafe in Seahouses …"

"I thought Bertrand was going mad. He looked all round the town but he couldn't find anywhere better."

"That man with the red braces who offered Bertrand the sauce to kill the taste of his spamburgers, and old Bertrand saying 'my dear fellow' …"

Beth drummed her feet on the turf in uncontrollable mirth. "You *mustn't* mock him," she spluttered.

Michael couldn't resist keeping her going.

"And my mother in the boat, asking if the captain's jumper was traditional-knit, and the captain saying he hadn't had nits for years."

Beth wondered whether you could die laughing.

"Where do you think Bertrand's gone now?" said Michael.

"To Alnwick, to buy that stuff for *Resurre*."

"I'm glad he took Sally. No more Glorororum."

"Yes, I'm getting a bit tired of Glororum myself. Where's your mother now? What's she doing?"

Mike raised his binoculars.

"Still on the landing-stage, giving the bird-warden hell.

in a corner."

"Complaining about the oil-pollution."

"Threat to our natural ecology … As if it was that poor sod's fault. But that's not really what she's narked about."

"What is, then?"

"The way they've roped off most of the island, so she can't walk on it." He changed his voice to impersonate his mother's.

"Young *man*! I have no objections to your fencing off the tern's nest-sites, but there are so many ropes I feel you've fenced off *me*!"

"I'll say one thing for you, Mike. You're fair. You're a bastard to *everybody*."

"I'm not a bastard to you."

"No, you aren't really. I often wonder why."

Silence. Mike buried his face in his binoculars. Beth wondered if he was blushing. But he just said, "Gannets!" explosively. "Cor, just look at 'em go. Wheeeh!"

Far out to sea, she caught the glint of white-and-yellow shapes diving.

"Don't hog the glasses, pig!"

Mike gave a fearful pig-snort, but he passed the binoculars over. Beth found the birds and held her breath.

"I'd like to do that – just fold my wings and dive straight into the water."

"Like a dive-bomber," said Mike.

"Like a Christian," said Beth.

"Like a *what*?"

"A Christian. Christians plunge from what they can see into what they can't. It's called having faith – it's dangerous."

"*Dangerous*!" Mike's voice rose to an incredulous squeak. "What's dangerous about being a Christian? Keep the heavenly Green Cross Code. God the Traffic-Warden. Keep off the grass – 'cos it's always greener on the other side. Same old hymns, same old prayers. Every week you ask God to help you do better – but you know bloody well you'll be back the following week saying, 'we have erred and strayed like lost sheep.' That's what Christians are – a flock of sheep. You can't imagine one going back the following week and saying, 'I've done bloody well this week, God – what about a little reward?'"

"I know what you mean. But I think Christianity's a bit like flying – it was marvellous and dangerous at the start, but people keep making it safer all the time. I mean the Wright brothers could see the ground ripping past and feel the wind in their hair, but now it's all Jumbo-jets and bad movies. The *old* Christians felt the wind in their hair. It wasn't easy, every-Sunday stuff then. Like Cuthbert living alone for years and dying on this rock."

Michael laughed.

"I like old Cuddy. He's great for annoying Bertrand with."

"Oh, it's useless talking seriously to you. Your only interest is annoying people. I'm going to look at the chapel."

"And I'm going to inspect the lighthouse. At least that does something *useful*."

They got up, glaring at each other. But once on their feet they found it difficult to part.

"It's too hot," said Beth. "And the chapel will smell of dogs I expect – old buildings always do. Let's go down to that pool and paddle."

The pool was shallow, but the water was just drinkable.

"Bet there's a dead sheep in it somewhere," said Mike. "Bet you die in screaming agony, drinking that."

"Oh, shut up." She splashed some water in his face. "Now you'll die in screaming agony too."

He splashed her back. They were still splashing when Madeleine arrived.

"Stop behaving like toddlers!" she snapped. "Do you know what that *stupid* bird-warden has just said to me?"

That was the end of peace.

45

X

When they got back to Monk's Heugh, Bertrand was already working. The area round *Resurre* was covered with mast and spars and sails, laid out so precisely that they made the trampled sand look like a workshop.

"That must have cost you a packet," said Madeleine. "And all for a fortnight's holiday."

Bertrand looked up, wiping sweat out of his eyes.

"It's my money."

"I suppose you've forgotten we need a new fridge when we get home?"

"I can mend the old one."

Madeleine tried a new tack.

"Do you know what that stupid bird-warden on the Farnes said to me?"

"I really want to get on with this, Madeleine."

"Well I'm going to make the tea. And if you're not all there when it's ready, it can sit and get cold. Don't expect me to call you." She swept off.

Beth watched her father. He was trying to screw a metal loop into *Resurre*'s gunwale, with a shining new patent tool. He looked very hot and very angry. Maybe it was Sally. She kept picking things off the sand and asking what they were for and not listening to the answers.

Beth put her arms round Sally, trying to distract her, but she wriggled free and picked up something else.

Mike moved in for a closer look.

"Get out of my light," snapped Bertrand. The sun was shining; there was plenty of light everywhere. But Bertrand hated being watched when he was working.

Then Beth realised somebody else was watching; from the

cliffpath. An old man with a bicycle. The bicycle was old and black, with huge wheels and not a glint of chrome anywhere. And though the evening was warm, the old man wore a blue overcoat and muffler. His trousers were tied up with string instead of bicycle-clips. It was hard to see his face under his cap.

Bertrand pulled savagely on the handle of the patent tool. The muscles of his back stood out like ropes, under his wet shirt. The tool gave a solitary click. Bertrand straightened up, and brushed the hair out of his eyes again.

"This wood's phenomenally hard. I'd never have believed it." He bent over the tool again. He was taking deep breaths to calm himself; his movements lacked their usual rhythm. Beth realised he must have been struggling with the boat for a long time.

Then there came, in the silence of hard breathing, a series of clicks. But it wasn't the tool. It was the old man descending the cliff. It was the freewheel of his bicycle clicking. He came and stood next to Beth. His hands on the handlebars were mottled with age. But his eyes watched the tool in Bertrand's hands with wrinkled intentness.

The tool gave one more click.

"Ye'll never manage it," said the old man. His voice was so broadly Northumbrian Beth could hardly understand him. But Bertrand heard. He looked up at the old man.

"What do you know about it?"

"Aah knaas," said the old man. "Yon's the Wind Eye's boat."

Bertrand braced himself for another effort. His feet ploughed great furrows in the sand as he searched for the best grip. Then his whole jaw, neck, back and arms locked into an iron pattern of muscles, the kind you see in biology books at school. The muscles stood out so hard that Beth gasped in fear.

There was a sharp crack as the patent tool snapped in half.

One jagged end glinted, then Bertrand was clutching his forearm. Blood trickled through his fingers.

"Aah telt you," said the old man. "Aah telt you that you wouldn't get the better o' the Wind Eye. But you wouldn't be telt."

"Get away!" shouted Bertrand. "This is *my* boat. This is *my* land. Get off it!"

The old man turned and slowly wheeled his bike up the cliff-path. The click of the freewheel was loud in the silence. Blood dripped from the tips of Bertrand's fingers onto the sand.

"Daddy, your arm!" said Beth. Bertrand looked at her without seeing her. Then he began picking up bits of equipment and throwing them into the black shed. The blood from his fingers made purple splotches on the new blue sail.

"I'll buy a concrete-drill tomorrow," he said. "That'll convince the Wind Eye creature, whoever *he* is."

"What'll you use for power?" asked Mike.

"I'll hire a generator, if I have to." He stalked ahead of them into the house.

Tea was not a cheerful meal. The baked beans were stone-cold. Bertrand refused to have his arm bandaged. Madeleine moaned about blood on the tablecloth. In the end, Bertrand said, "Let's go to the cinema in Alnwick."

But the cinema wasn't a success either. It was a rather silly Western in which fourteen people got shot. The children would have enjoyed it, only they knew how Bertrand felt about stupid Westerns. They saw it through his eyes, knew what he would say afterwards.

"It's the brainlessness of it I can't stand," he said, as they turned onto the Bamburgh road. "Every time the plot started to sag, they killed somebody off. Some of the people that got killed hadn't had the chance to say a thing; they were just dragged in to get killed.

"And it's so unreal. The hero gets shot in the shoulder and he just ties a handkerchief round it and carries on being quick-on-the-draw. Do you know what happens if a man really gets hit in the shoulder by a forty-five slug? It throws him ten yards and nearly tears his shoulder off – he's a cripple for life."

"Stop talking like that," said Madeleine. "You'll upset the children. All this talk about shoulders being torn off – you're more violent than the film."

"I, violent?" yelped Bertrand. "I wouldn't hurt a fly. I've been against violence all my life. I'm a *pacifist*; one of the original founders of Ban-the-Bomb."

"You're the most violent man I know. Of course you won't admit it. You're scared of it, so you won't face it in yourself."

Bertrand crashed the Volvo down into third gear, and drove so hard up a hill that the engine screamed.

"I'm totally opposed to violence because violence solves nothing."

"You're being violent right now."

"Oh, I can't talk to you – you're utterly unreasonable."

He drove the rest of the journey in controlled careful silence. Which gave Madeleine all the time in the world to tell the whole family just what the stupid birdwarden on Farne had said to her.

"Death where is thy sting ..." muttered Michael between clenched teeth.

Beth was glad to get to bed; but she couldn't relax. Perhaps it was the heat. Suddenly Northumberland was not living up to its two-sweaters-in-August reputation. Or perhaps it was the name that old man had used.

The Wind Eye. What did it mean? What *could* it mean? Probably she had mis-heard the old man; his accent was thick enough. But, on the fringes of sleep, the name stuck in her mind like a fish-hook. She kept on remembering the huge Northumbrian sky that forever looked down on you, making you feel like a fly on tablecloth. And the wind that was always blowing here ... She tossed and turned, trying to find cool places in the sheets. Finally she dozed off, hand clenched under her pillow.

She wakened with a sense of something wrong. Moonlight was streaming across the room onto Sally's bed. The bedclothes were thrown back and it was empty.

She called softly, "Sally, Sally." No reply. Had she gone outside to the loo? Usually Beth made sure she went before bed, but tonight she'd forgotten.

She was groping for her dressing-gown when a slight movement in the room made her turn. Sally was standing at the window in her nightdress, outlined against the moon. Beth ran to her, full of relief.

"Sally! Silly old Sally. Why didn't you answer me?"

Sally still didn't answer. When Beth turned her round, her eyes were blank. Then she recognised Beth and smiled.

"Wasn't the singing lovely, Beth?"

"What singing?"

"The singing in the sky. From the moonbeams and the fiery ball. Didn't you see?"

"Of course not. You dreamt it. And you've been sleep walking again. You were hanging out of the window – you could have fallen."

"I was hanging out watching the fiery ball – over there." Sally pointed towards the Farnes.

"Back to bed. No more singing."

Sally looked sad. "My hand hurts." She put her thumb in her mouth.

"Oh you *silly*. You've been wearing your glove in bed again. No wonder your hand's itchy."

In the daytime Sally always wore a glove on her bad hand, with a hole for the uninjured thumb to stick out. But if you didn't watch her, she wore it in bed as well. In hot weather the glove made the hand itch.

Beth said, "I'll put some camomile lotion on it." She peeled the glove off.

Much though she loved Sally, Beth hated touching the bad hand. Even in the dark she could feel its iron shrunkenness; the layers of scar-tissue that constantly peeled off to reveal more layers of scar-tissue.

"There! That better?"

"Mmm," said Sally, but her thumb went back into her mouth. Still, the camomile must have worked, for Beth soon heard her snores.

She still couldn't sleep herself; she was worried. It was all right saying Sally had heard the singing in her dreams, but if those dreams started her sleepwalking again, and she sleepwalked out of the upstairs window …

She didn't want to worry Bertrand with it; not at the moment especially. He thought people talked a lot of rubbish about dreams. But he'd have to be told.

She told him while they were washing-up the breakfast things together. She could hear Sally glororuming upstairs. Madeleine was hanging out washing at the bottom of the garden and Mike was throwing sticks at a bottle on the fence.

Bertrand frowned.

"What time was this?"

"About three o'clock. Her hand was itching again; perhaps that caused it. I put some camomile on, but it's worse this morning."

"We'd better take her to the doctor's."

Beth sighed inwardly. All those endless trips to the doctor's. They did no good. Except to ease Bertrand's conscience.

"I'll have a word with her. *Sally!*" he shouted up the stairs. She came down still sucking the thumb.

"What's all this about sleepwalking, young lady?"

"I wasn't. I was awake. I heard them singing. It was *angels*."

"Nonsense. You were dreaming."

"I wasn't. I pinched myself and it *hurt*."

"You *dreamed* you pinched yourself. You *dreamed* it hurt."

"I didn't. It was angels carrying a soul up to Heaven."

Bertrand's mouth tightened. He gripped Sally by the shoulders with a terrifying gentleness.

"I've told you before. Dreams are just our minds going on working while we're asleep. Thinking about what's happened during the day."

"It wasn't. It was *angels*."

"For God's sake, Bertrand, leave the child alone. She's only six. Let her enjoy her childhood while she can."

Madeleine was standing in the doorway, a pair of wet socks over her arm and the light of battle in her eyes.

"Don't tell me how to bring up my child."

"I should have thought after what you did to that hand of hers, you'd have a bit more humility."

There was a horrible silence. Madeleine had mentioned the unmentionable.

Mike, peering over his mother's shoulder, caught Beth's eye and flicked his own towards the door. Beth needed no prodding. She picked up Sally bodily and moved to follow him. Madeleine made way for them, never taking her eyes off Bertrand for a second.

They were not out of earshot when the row started.

An hour later, Madeleine swept out, jumped into the Spitfire and roared off for an unknown destination.

A quarter of an hour after that, Bertrand came out, looking calm but rather ill.

"Come on, Beth, Sally. If we leave it any longer, we'll miss morning surgery."

*

The doctor wore brown tweeds and had a quiet brown face. With his balding forehead, sad eyes and drooping moustache he looked a bit like that portrait of William Shakespeare.

When he'd examined Sally's hand he said, "I prescribe lime-juice for both the young ladies. If they'll have a word with my receptionist …"

The receptionist, a motherly soul, took Sally off to the kitchen to supervise the mixing of the drinks. Beth sat down on a waiting-room chair and leaned her head wearily back against the hardboard partition. It was very thin; she could hear every word that was being said in the surgery.

She dreaded hearing it again. Every doctor asked the same question, and Bertrand could never give a short answer. He always flayed himself publicly, as he was doing now. But somehow Beth always had to listen.

"We had bought an electric fire. With a fireguard of course. Sally was only two at the time. She was fascinated by the electric bars; she was always switching them on, to see them light up. My wife – my first wife – wanted to get rid of the fire. But we'd only just got it and it hadn't been cheap. The guard seemed quite adequate. I said Sally was just showing a natural curiosity. She couldn't get more than a blister off the guard, and that would teach her the danger of fire.

"Anyway, I was upstairs one day, when I heard her start screaming. I ran down so fast I fell and twisted my ankle. I had to crawl the rest of the way. She'd prised the fireguard apart with the poker. It was actually trapping her hand against the bars."

There was a short silence. Doctors always flinched at that point.

"Have you tried …"

"Every specialist in Harley Street."

Another short silence.

"Incurable," the doctor said. "Meanwhile, there's this surface irritation caused by the glove in hot weather. It could become chronic. Why don't you leave the glove off altogether?"

"And have everyone staring at her? Or trying hard to be nice and not to stare? How could she make friends with everyone flinching away? Sometimes I think she'd be better off socially with a complete amputation of the hand."

The doctor sighed, then Beth could hear his pen scratching.

"Some stronger ointment, a new formula. And a sedative to help the sleepwalking. *That's* more worrying, really."

"My eldest daughter sleeps in the same room; she can keep an eye on her."

The doctor came out and had a lime-juice with them, and told Sally about the seals that lived on the Farnes. He gave Beth a sad smile. He was a nice man.

XI

The polythene bottle, bobbing in the surf, made a nice target. Hard to hit. But Mike was too good. After he had hit it for the tenth time, he got bored. He wandered up the beach and stared at *Resurre*.

What a flop! He examined the place where Bertrand had tried to drill his hole. There was a tiny dent. But Bertrand's patent tool had literally torn apart, and it wasn't Hong Kong rubbish either. German. If the Germans couldn't cope with *Resurre*, nobody could. She'd never sail now.

What a rotten holiday. So promising, with those cosmic islands, and yet everything turned sour. How had Uncle Henry stood twenty years in this horrible dump?

Uncle Henry ... This must have been Henry's boat. He must have sailed it at some time. Or perhaps he only rowed it. Therefore, Q.E.D., the oars for *Resurre* must be somewhere in the black shed.

God, what a sweat, hauling out all that lumber again on a morning like this. But he always felt better for doing something, especially when Beth wasn't around. Heaven knew when any of his potty family would return.

So he started. He thought he'd use a burrowing technique, to save moving all the stuff. He crawled into the hot tarry darkness with his torch, working as much by feel as anything.

Three times he squirmed through to the back wall. Sharp objects poked him in the ribs. Cobwebs wound themselves round his eyes and ears. Once he thought he was really stuck. And each time he got into a panic on the way out of the cramped sweating dark. It was good to stand on the beach taking in the wide blueness of the sea, letting the wind blow cool on his wet shirt.

The fourth time, his hands found something long and round. When he got it out, he saw it was an oar, large and clumsy, with a broad blade. He left it on the sand and went back to look for the other one. It wasn't there.

He kicked his find disconsolately. Even Henry would keep oars in pairs. What good was one stupid oar? He tried it in the rowlocks of the boat. It didn't even fit.

Then he noticed a third rowlock towards the back. It was a single rowlock, on the right-hand side. The oar fitted; it was a steering-oar. Like the Egyptians, and the Greeks, and the Vikings used. *Resurre* looked much more like a working proposition, with the steering-oar in place. But mere rowing-boats didn't need a steering-oar; so there *must* be sails.

He went back to Monk's Heugh quivering with excitement. It was still empty and silent. He drank a pint of milk straight out of the bottle, cut bread an inch thick and a piece of cheese nearly as large, and went back to consider.

He had groped all over the shed; felt everything *likely*. Now he must look for something *unlikely*.

And on the next groping journey he found it. A large bundle wrapped in tarpaulin. When he tried lifting it, things creaked and moved right to the back of the shed. So it was very long.

It took half-an-hour to work it free, but it was worth it. The tarpaulin unrolled to reveal a mast and a tapering spar, and a lot of tarry cord. It had the same ancient bleached look as *Resurre* itself. And the tarpaulin turned out to be a sail, patched and salt-stained.

A fever seized him. He must have the sail up before Bertrand returned. Otherwise Bertrand would start being bossy and something would go wrong. Anyway, it was his boat, not Bertrand's. He'd found it.

It wasn't hard to see how it worked. There were holes for the mast in the midship seat, and the floorboards below. Then all he had to do was tie the ropes that dangled from the mast to the holes in *Resurre*'s bow and sides. The tapering spar was hauled up the mast by a rope through the mast-top, and the sail was already attached to the spar.

He stood back. His finger-tips were sore from the coarse tarpaulin and splinters from the wood, but he'd done it. A light wind came, and bellied out the sail, and *Resurre* looked very like a Viking ship, as her hull rocked restlessly on the sand. Except the sail was so small. There was a rag of pennant on top to show how the wind blew. He felt he would burst with excitement.

"Clever boy!" It was Beth's voice. It made him jump a foot in the air. He hadn't even heard the car return.

"It *is* a Viking-ship," said Sally, as if that settled the matter.

"No it's not," said Bertrand. "It's a balanced lug-sail rig. Often used for small fishing-craft. Quite typical, if rather small."

"Can we sail her?" asked Beth, breathlessly. Bertrand walked round the boat, kicking and pulling at things rather spitefully; but nothing fell off.

"I suppose so. She'll be terribly slow, and bound to leak; to begin with at any rate. We'd better take the oars from the sailing-dinghy. And lifejackets, everybody."

"I'll make some sandwiches," said Beth. "We can have a picnic on board. Come and help, Mike."

When they got back, Bertrand had untied and retied all Mike's knots, though they'd been perfectly good boy-scout variety.

But it was impossible to be narky, as they pushed *Resurre* down to the sea. It was uncannily easy to push her round hull across the sand, in spite of her weight. It was almost as if she wanted to go. She floated in the low breakers as predictably as a pendulum.

"She's dry as a bone," said Beth.

"And not hard to get aboard," said Mike. "Not like that bloody dinghy."

"Be fair," said Bertrand. "It's a different kind of morning – much calmer. And you'll miss the dinghy after a bit. This boat will be as exciting as a pram."

So she proved. They sailed sedately to port, and then back to starboard. Objects on the beach hardly seemed to move. They ate their sandwiches in comfort. Mike got bored.

"Can't we take her out a bit further?"

Bertrand shrugged.

"Why not?" He put the steering-oar over; the shore receded.

"That's funny," said Beth. "I didn't realise it was misty." The shore had vanished.

"Damn," said Bertrand. "I never thought we'd require a compass. Back to the beach! If we keep the wind on our right cheeks, we'll soon be there. The Farnes are notorious for these mists."

He put the boat about. The sea-mist closed in further. They could see no more than a circle of waves twenty feet across, but *Resurre* cradled them so gently it was impossible to be worried.

After a long time, Bertrand glanced at his watch.

"Fifteen minutes. We should have been on the beach ten minutes ago. Even this antique can't be as slow as that." And indeed, *Resurre* didn't seem to be going slowly. Her sail was drawing well, and a modest foam bubbled at the bows.

"Perhaps we ought to turn round," said Beth.

"Don't be ridiculous," said Bertrand sharply. "If we do, we'll sail straight out to sea. You don't think the wind-and-wave pattern reverse because a mist comes down, do you? We *must* be heading for the shore."

They sailed for another fifteen minutes. The sea-mist receded a little; *Resurre* seemed to go a little faster, and that was all. Everyone was straining their eyes and ears and noses.

"Doesn't it smell *lovely*," said Sally. They all sniffed. Mike shrugged.

"Seaweed, salt. Same as usual."

"But it does smell lovely," said Beth. "Clean. Perhaps it's something missing, that we are used to smelling. Like air-pollution."

"Air-pollution?" scoffed Mike. "We're not in Huddersfield, you know. If any air's clean, it's here."

"A mistaken supposition," said Bertrand. "Scientists have proved that with a west wind, the pollution from Tees-side chemical-works drifts as far as Sweden."

"Good lord," said Mike in an awed voice. "Look!" Everyone peered over the side. *Resurre*'s sharp bow was parting a positive raft of puffins. They did not fly away; just paddled their feet enough to avoid the boat. Sally leaned out and nearly managed to stroke one.

"That's funny," said Mike. "You know when Madeleine told us about the bird-warden on Farne?"

Everyone groaned.

"Well, *she* said that *he* said that there were hardly any puffins left round Farne, because of pollution. He ought to see this, the stupid burke! And so tame; the ones we saw from the trip-boat flew away before we could get near them."

"That's the advantage of sail," said Bertrand. "No noisy motor to alarm them." The puffins faded away into the mist.

"What's that?" said Beth.

"What's what?"

"Thought I heard a bell."

"There are no bell-buoys in these waters," said Bertrand. "You are starting to imagine you hear things, because you can't see anything."

"It sounded more like a *church*-bell."

"What, on a Tuesday afternoon?"

"Bell-ringing practice?"

"Even bell-ringers have to go to work."

"I heard a bell too," said Sally, putting her thumb in her mouth.

"In that case please be quiet, all of you, and let's listen," said Bertrand with an edge in his voice.

Beth went off into a dream. Perhaps they were caught in a circular bubble of mist that would move round them forever …

"Land," said Bertrand suddenly. There was a sound of waves breaking on rock, and a dim shape in the mist to port. "We must have been sailing nearly parallel to the coast. The wind must have veered after all."

Suddenly everyone was talking at once.

"Lor," said Mike. "It's *cliffs* – they must be eighty feet high."

"That's impossible," said Bertrand. "There are no cliffs this high for ten miles either way."

"Except the Farnes," said Mike. "This *is* the Farnes. Look at those nesting birds." They all peered up at a towering rock-stack.

"Guillemots," said Bertrand. "But they can't be nesting. It's the wrong season. The young birds are fully-fledged by now."

"I can bloody see them! Look for yourself. Up there. I can see the chicks opening their bills to be fed."

"Nonsense," snapped Bertrand. "But you're right about this being the Farnes. The wind must have veered right round, and we're in trouble. So shut up and *listen*."

At that moment, a rock loomed straight ahead, with waves washing over it. Bertrand forced the helm right over and *Resurre* scraped past, too close for comfort. Bertrand began to sweat, in spite of the mist.

"The problem is, which of the Farnes is it?" He spoke almost to himself. "We'd better keep these cliffs in sight, till we recognize a lighthouse or landmark. Then we'll know where we are."

It was tricky, keeping the cliffs just in sight and yet missing the rocks, in a strange boat. It was one of the times when Mike admired Bertrand.

"Yoohoo!" Sally was standing up in the bow, waving wildly. She made everybody jump.

"Sit down, Sally," said Bertrand crossly.

"But I saw a *man*. He waved to us. Didn't *you* see him?" Everyone looked at her blankly. Her lip quivered.

"No more fairy-stories, Sally," said Bertrand.

"It wasn't! There was a little beach, and a man standing on it, waving."

"We could do with a beach," said Bertrand. "Till the fog lifts." He put the steering-oar over, and sure enough, a beach appeared. *Resurre* ran gently aground, and everyone said "Whew".

"Young children have the sharpest eyes because they have the emptiest minds," said Bertrand, which was a bit rough on Sally. After all she *had* found the beach.

They sat for a long time, rocking gently as the waves moved the stern of the boat.

"Can't we explore?" asked Mike.

Bertrand looked doubtful. "It's undoubtedly a bird-sanctuary, and out of bounds. Besides, you could fall down the cliff in this mist."

"Oh, for Pete's sake!"

"All right, but keep together."

The climb off the beach was easy; there was even a path. The first thing they saw was the dead trunk of a tree, with one stump of branch.

"There's your *man*, Sally!"

"But, Daddy, it isn't. He had a bald head; he *waved* to me."

"Trick of the light." They turned left, and started round the cliffs.

"It's an extensive island," said Bertrand, "with grass and

plants. That means it's either Inner Farne, Brownsman or Staple – the rest are just bare rocks. If it's Farne, we'll see the lighthouse soon."

"There are no trees on Inner Farne," said Mike.

"Depends what you call a tree," panted Beth, as they stumbled past a gnarled specimen ten foot high. "Is that a tree or a bush?"

"There are no trees *anywhere* in the Farnes. They were felled in Anglo-Saxon times, and never recovered," shouted Bertrand, back out of the mist. "Don't lag behind."

"Does he ever give up knowing it all?" whispered Mike.

"Never," whispered Beth. She giggled and took Michael's hand, and then abruptly took Sally's hand as well.

"There *was* a man. He *waved* to me," said Sally defiantly.

They walked round three corners of the island. There was no lighthouse. There was no Prior Castell's tower, or Cuthbert's chapel.

They saw a low round wall, which Bertrand dismissed as a sheepfold, and a quaint box of driftwood and fabric poised over a deep sea-filled chasm, which Bertrand said was a bird-watching hide, and in a most dangerous place, too. He would ring up the bird-warden and report it.

Then they were back at the beach again. It was good to see *Resurre*.

"Not a sign of human habitation," said Bertrand. "So this island must be Staple. Even Brownsman's got a cottage on it, and the remains of a lighthouse." He made a great play of drawing diagrams in the sand, and holding up a wet finger to test the wind. "This mist isn't lifting, but at least we've got a bearing. If we keep the wind on our *left* cheeks, that will take us north-west and home."

Which is what they did. When they broke out of the mist they were opposite Budle Bay.

"Well done, Daddy," said Beth warmly.

"Half-a-mile too far north," said Bertrand modestly.

"Inexplicable, that." He turned *Resurre* to sail down the coast. Just as they were about to land, a red-sailed *Enterprise* passed them.

"Like your boat," shouted the helmsman, who was smoking a pipe. "Quite a curiosity. Nice day for a sail, isn't it?"

"Don't go too far out," shouted Bertrand. "There's a tricky mist round the Farnes."

"Really?" The man's pipe waggled violently and his eyebrows shot up. "That's odd. I've had them clear in view the last two hours."

They looked, and there were the islands, basking like long seals in the sun, the lighthouse and white patch on Inner Farne gleaming.

"Ah well, sailing's not for fools," said the helmsman, and shot off, waggling his pipe still.

"Silly idiot," said Bertrand. "You can't warn some people."

After they'd snugged-down *Resurre* they straggled across the dunes. Mike sat down suddenly on the last dune.

"What's the matter?" asked Beth.

"Funny about that mist, wasn't it – I mean the other yachtsman not seeing it?"

"Yes."

"I'll tell you something funnier. That island we landed on – it *was* Inner Farne, you know. It wasn't Staple."

"Oh, Mike ..."

"That beach – don't you remember it from landing in the trip-boat yesterday? Same pattern of rock-strata."

"But all the islands have the same rock-strata."

"O.K. then. But what about that cliff we saw with the guillemots? There was one rock-stack, wasn't there – one big pillar standing out of the sea, all on its own?"

"Yes."

"Well Staple hasn't got one rock-stack. It's got three, all in a row, you couldn't miss 'em. And there *were* young birds in those nests, in spite of what Bertrand says."

"Go on, you can't see things properly in a mist."

"There were young birds, I tell you."

"Oh, you're being ridiculous. Anything to prove my father's wrong."

Mike gave her an oddly pitying look.

"Well if that's what you think, I'm off for tea."

XII

Something like a cold hand passed across Beth's brow. She snuggled deeper into the blankets, but the cold hand would not go away. Reluctantly she woke up.

Her watch said 3 a.m., and immediately she looked across the moonlit room to Sally's bed. It was empty again.

She turned to the window, but Sally wasn't there either.

"Oh, Sally!"

Then she realised what the cold hand had been: a strong draught was coming through the open bedroom door. She got up and went out into the corridor. The draught was blowing up the staircase. The front door was open.

Her first impulse was to run for Bertrand. But Sally might just be at the loo – get her back to bed quickly and no harm done.

Beth stepped out into the sandy garden. It had been raining, and the rain had smoothed the sand flat. Except in one place where small feet had broken through the wet surface to the dry sand beneath. Small footsteps led away in the direction of the sea.

"Oh, Sally!" Beth turned back to the house in an agony of indecision. If she fetched Bertrand, she'd lose five minutes with explanations when Sally might be in danger this very minute.

She looked up at Bertrand's bedroom window, gave one mighty screech of "Daddy!", waited till a torch went on behind the curtains, then started running.

Sally's tracks meandered through the lower dunes, turning this way and that, as if she was searching for something. Several times Beth thought she'd lost them, before she broke out onto the open beach. The waves were running four feet high, throwing up a fine spray that drifted inland like smoke. The moonlight played tricks with the spray, making little rainbows of blue and green that vanished and reappeared. Sally's footprints were visible in the wet sand, but the incoming tide was starting to wash them away.

Beth ran until her nightdress mounted to her waist, until her lungs were pumping and a pain grew in her side. Three times she thought she saw a white flicker by the very edge of the surf, but she could not be sure.

And then she saw Sally, up to her waist in the foam, her nightie floating round her.

"Sally!" she screamed. But the child didn't turn. Instead, she took several steps further into the sea. Beth splashed after her, picked her up bodily and carried her to shore. The small body was icy-cold and the blue eyes would not focus. Beth shook her violently.

"Hello, Beth. Have you come to see the man?"

"Which man?"

"In the sea. Look!"

Beth followed her pointing finger; she could see nothing but white-horses in the moonlight.

"*What* man, you little ninny?"

"The man I saw on the island. The man who waved, with the bald head. He came to my window and waved again. So I went down to see him. But when I got there he was going away. I followed him, but I couldn't catch up. Then he took off his beach-robe, and he waded right into the sea, up to his *arms*. And he was singing a song. Then he came out again, but he didn't dry himself. He knelt down and went on singing. Then two little sort of dogs came – long little bendy dogs – and they played round his feet while he was singing. So he stopped singing and sent them away. Then he went back into the sea again, and then you came. It was ever so lovely. I wanted to talk to him and ask what the dogs were."

Fear made Beth screech like a fishwife.

"Little idiot. There isn't any man! You've been sleepwalking again. *Dreaming*."

"No I haven't. There was a man. There's his robe."

Beth's heart gave a thud. There was a garment lying on the sand. She walked towards it, quivering all over and holding her breath.

But it was just a lump of old sacking, washed up by the tide, damp and falling apart in her hand. The kind of thing you find on any beach.

There was shouting behind. The beam of a torch made the speargrass on the dunes stand out black.

"That's Daddy. Please don't tell him about the man, Sally. He won't believe you, and there'll only be another row."

Sally gave her a conspiratorial look, and pressed her lips together. In another minute they were in the thick of their whole pyjama-clad family.

But Bertrand wasn't cross, just worried.

"There's just one solution to this caper," he said. "New locks on all the doors and windows. Sally-proof locks, eh?" He picked up his younger daughter and poked her with affection. "Sally-proof locks from Alnwick, first thing in the morning."

They set off back to the house, laughing and joking as people do when some disaster has been averted.

All except Beth, trailing behind. Something was nagging at her mind. A smell. What smell?

The smell of that lump of old sacking washed up by the tide.

It had the same smell as … the boots in the attache case under her bed. The boots somebody had thrown over a cliff. The boots Uncle Henry had hidden in the attache case with that strange note.

Had there really been a man outside the window tonight, waving to Sally? A strange wild filthy old man? Had he come back for his boots?

Don't be stupid, she told herself. All old decaying things smell the same. It was just a dustbin-smell. Pull yourself together, girl.

All the same, she'd take Mike's advice, and throw the case away in the morning. That would settle it. It did make a nasty smell in the middle of the night. She didn't know why she'd kept it as long as she had.

But in the morning she forgot all about it.

XIII

"Let's have a sail," said Mike.

Beth yawned. The sun was warm, and the sand was warm. Bertrand had gone to Alnwick. Madeleine was rattling the breakfast washing-up, in a guilt-making way, through the open kitchen window. But Beth felt like sunbathing and catching up on sleep.

"Daddy won't let us sail without him."

"He only meant the sailing-dinghy. He won't mind if we go in *Resurre*. He said she was as safe as a pram."

"That mist …"

"That wasn't *Resurre*'s fault. Anyway, it won't happen two days running. Look how clear it is!" He raised his binoculars. "I can see the bird-warden on Farne lighting his pipe."

Beth laughed. "Liar!"

"C'mon. The tide's up. We won't have to drag *Resurre* five yards."

"C'mon, lazy," said Sally, pulling her by the other arm.

Beth gave in. She could always sunbathe in the boat,.

"We won't go far," she said.

"No, we won't go far, I promise," said Mike. Beth frowned. That sounded a typical Mike-promise; his voice was much more excited than it should have been. But she'd agreed to go now.

Once afloat, she wondered what she'd been worried about. The waves had dropped overnight; so had the wind. If anything, *Resurre* was more cradle-like than ever. She could hardly keep her eyes open.

"Hey, there's a bottle in the sea out there," said Mike. "Might have a message in it." Sally's eyes lit up, as he knew they would.

"Don't tease her, Michael," said Beth. But she put the steering-oar over, and headed for the bottle.

Before they reached it, the mist came down.

"That's *it*," said Beth. "Home we go." But the mist was getting rapidly darker. Before she could turn the boat, it was black as pitch.

"Going to be a thunderstorm," said Sally smugly. She loved thunderstorms.

"It can't be. It's too dark," gasped Beth, fighting the oar. "It must be an eclipse or something." Her only thought was to get back to the beach and indoors.

Then the mist cleared, and they were sailing through a calm moonlit night.

Beth shut her eyes three times, but when she opened them, it was still a calm moonlit night. Her mind was making wild kangaroo-leaps to no purpose. Sally was clinging to her, whimpering.

"I want to go home. Take me home, Beth. Take me home! I want DADDY!"

"Oh, Mike, where are we? What shall I *do*?" Panic swirled up like vomit in Beth's throat.

Michael chuckled, like someone playing a harmless joke. It was an oddly soothing sound. He took the steering oar and turned for the shore.

Mist, then the beach and bright sunlight, and Madeleine hanging out a teacloth in the garden. Beth had never been so glad to see Madeleine in her life.

"Mike, what *happened*?"

He smiled knowingly. "Shall we try it again?"

"No! Not till you tell me what it is."

"Can't you see? This boat's a time-machine. Like the *Tardis* in 'Doctor Who'."

"Michael, don't be *completely* ridiculous."

"All right, *you* explain what we've just seen, then."

She was silent.

"I'm serious, you know," said Mike. "I worked it out after our trip with Bertrand yesterday. We sailed into mist round the Farnes – but that yachtsman said there hadn't been any mist round the Farnes; he thought we were potty.

"And that island we landed on. It was Inner Farne. Inner Farne without a lighthouse where there should have been a lighthouse. Inner Farne with trees where there shouldn't have been any trees. Therefore, Q.E.D., an Inner Farne from another time. And since your father says Farne hasn't had trees since Anglo-Saxon times, perhaps we travelled back that far."

"But why should this ship be a time-machine?"

Michael shrugged. "Who knows? But she must be pretty old. Perhaps she can go back to any time she's known. I can't see her travelling forward into the space-age somehow, poor old thing."

"But …"

"Look, I'm not Bertrand! I don't claim to know all the answers. I just like having fun. So what are we going to do, sit here wallowing all day?" He indicated the open sea. "It didn't look very dangerous out there, did it?"

"I'm as brave as *you* are," flared Beth.

"Prove it, then."

Beth took the steering oar. It wasn't so scaring the second time. The moonlit sea was calm and beautiful, though the air made them shiver.

"Feel the water," said Mike. "Twenty degrees colder at least. Wish I'd brought my anorak." He peered about him, through his binoculars, as calm as if he was on a bird-watching trip.

"You all right, love?" said Beth to Sally. The child huddled close and sucked her thumb, but she said, "Mmm." Beth noticed *Resurre* was not standing still. She was moving gently towards where the Farnes were etched inky-black.

"Hey, Mike, there's two lights on Inner Farne. D'you think it's a lighthouse?"

Mike looked hard through his binoculars.

"No … The lights are moving about. I think it's people with torches. Let's go see."

Resurre slid forward a little faster, but very peacefully.

"That lovely clean smell's back, Mike."

"That's my girl. I knew you'd enjoy it. Hey, there are more lights up north. On Holy Island. Must be a big night for someone."

As they came in under the lee of Farne, the torches on the island passed out of sight. The other lights on Holy Island vanished too. They were left feeling oddly at a loss, yet reluctant to go home, like guests after a good party. It smelt so happy, in spite of the cold.

"Dawn's coming up," said Mike. And indeed the rocks of Farne were becoming clearer every minute. You could see the little stunted trees on top, leaning away from the north-east wind.

The sun showed above the rim of the horizon, and the rocks of Farne shone red in its light.

"Oh, look!" squealed Sally. "Oh, *do* look!" They looked. All around them, solemnly watching, rose the heads of seals.

"There must be hundreds," whispered Beth.

"They look like the Urban District Council," said Mike. "All bald heads and droopy moustaches."

"What are they all waiting for?"

"For you to make a speech, dear." Mike got up and threw out one arm.

"Friends, Romans, countrymen …"

"Please don't fool about," said Beth. "Don't insult them. They look too sad, somehow."

"Oh, you soppy ha'porth. Seals always look like that. Have you ever seen one laughing?" But he sat down, and they waited.

Suddenly Beth said, "They're all looking towards Inner Farne." It was true. Every seal's head was turned towards the island.

"What are they watching? There's nothing there."

"There's ripples in the water," said Mike. "They're watching the ripples. They're the kind a boat makes – but there's no boat. Hell, it must be a shark or whale or something – heading straight for us. Let's get out of here."

But he was too late. As the strange ripples surrounded her, *Resurre* began to move north of her own volition. The vast crowd of seals closed in round them, swimming strongly and every so often casting their sorrowful eyes at the boat. And the air was full of seabirds: herring-gulls and black-backed gulls, and Sandwich terns with their long streaming tails, keeping perfect station above them and filling the dawn with their plaintive cries.

"We surrender – we'll come quietly," shouted Mike, trying to make a joke of it. Neither Beth nor Sally replied. Tears were streaming down Beth's face, and Sally was staring bewildered at the floorboards in the middle of the boat. Mike felt horribly alone, shut out.

"Hey, you two! Say something!"

But they stayed silent. Mike fidgeted; he liked a bit of action personally. But action there was none, except the boat drawing ever-nearer to Holy Island. He could see a miserable collection of thatched huts by the shore, surrounded by a circular stone wall … looked like a pig-farm or something. And in front … he glanced through his binoculars … a big crowd of blokes standing silent on the beach … a reception committee … wow!

In a panic at the silence, he leapt to the stern and grabbed the steering-oar out of Beth's hands.

Resurre came up into the wind. Her sail flogged from side to side, wildly. By the time he got things under control, *Resurre* was heading south, and the birds and seals were gone.

"Oh, what've you spoiled it for?" said Beth. "It was so lovely – like a funeral, only happy as well."

"What was? All I saw was a lot of bloody seals and birds, and the local yokels standing on the shore looking nasty."

"Oh, Mike! You *peasant*!"

"What do you mean, peasant?"

Sally's voice broke through the quarrel.

"Why was he lying down, Beth? Was he asleep? Why were his hands crossed on his chest?"

"Who, love?"

"The bald man; the one that waved to me on the beach. He was lying down in the middle of the boat, with his arms crossed on his chest round a little box." She pointed to the empty floorboards at Mike's feet.

Mike shuddered. "Let's get back to the present day, for Pete's sake. I want my lunch, or should it be breakfast?"

They came out of the mist into mid-day. Madeleine was standing by the garden fence shouting "Lu–unch".

"Oh, there you are. Where'd you get to? I couldn't see you anywhere. Bertrand was just starting to flap."

Mike put his finger to his lips. The other two nodded.

XIV

After lunch, the sun got even hotter. Beth lay on the sand by the garden-gate, soaking it in. Peaceful.

"Hey," said Madeleine, standing over her so that Beth felt the cool of her shadow. "Hey, I'm going into Alnwick. I've got a funny feeling about that boat of yours; and I'm going to check up on something. I don't think you should sail it again till I get back. O.K?"

"Mmm," said Beth sleepily. All she wanted to do was to lie there, digesting Madeleine's bacon-and-beans and the fantastic events of the morning. If she lay and dreamt and thought, it might all sort itself out. Her mind might stop leaping between panic and a strange happiness.

But peace was denied. Michael flopped down beside her.

"What was Mum on about?"

"She's gone to Alnwick. She said we weren't to sail *Resurre* again till she came back."

"Did she? And what bloody business is it of hers? You can't do a *thing* without her poking her nose in."

Beth yawned. "She's got a funny feeling about it."

"She gets funny feelings about everything. She's just trying to spoil things, you know. We'd better get another sail in while we still can."

"Leave it, Mike."

"Like hell I will. It's my turn to have some fun this afternoon."

Beth sat up crossly.

"What do you mean, *you* have some fun?"

"I mean this time, I'll steer her."

"What difference would that make?"

"I've been working it out. When you steered her, what

happened? Lots of dickie-birds and dear sad seals and happy funerals and you weeping buckets. I mean, it was all so *you*; so like your bloody daydreams. No action. Honestly, I was bored stiff."

"You mean I made it all happen with my mind?"

"No, I don't think you made it happen. I mean *Resurre* showed you a piece of the past that you would like. But if I steer her, she'll show me something I'd like."

"Such as?"

"Just you wait and see."

She didn't like the smile on his face; it was the Madeleine-smile, the one that meant trouble.

"Go on your own!"

"Sally's coming with me."

"She's *not*."

"She's waiting in the boat already. She can't get enough of it." He sniggered.

"Don't be vulgar." But she got up wearily. She'd better be there, just in case.

The waves were cold, grey and high. They appeared out of the mist like ghosts, and then hit the boat with breath-taking force. Beth cuddled Sally in close; the wind was icy, and she was glad they'd brought anoraks.

Mike was whistling to himself cheerfully. He had a plastic Woolworth's carrier-bag at his feet, full of rounded pebbles about three inches long; his favourite ammunition on any beach.

"What've you brought those for?"

"Just you wait and see. Hey, she's going a bomb, isn't she? Old Bertrand was wrong about her being slow."

Beth looked. Certainly *Resurre* was going faster than she ever had before.

"Bet I could make her do ten knots," said Mike, "but not now. We'd better go steady."

"Why?"

"Listen! Smell!"

She listened and smelled. Through the mist came a creaking that wasn't *Resurre*. A creaking of rope and leather. And a foul smell. A slum smell with a whiff of butcher's shop in it. And then the sound of singing, full of grunts.

"What is it, Mike?"

"What I've been looking for. Vikings!"

"Oh, no!" She didn't scoff. The smell and noises were nasty enough to be anything. She tried to grab the steering-oar, but Mike pushed her away.

"Steady, fool. You'll have us into them. We're sailing alongside; they don't know we're here."

Beth stared into the mist wildly. The palest shadow of a low boat with a huge sail showed for a second, and faded.

"We're going *home*!" She made another grab for the oar.

"It's all right," said Mike. "They can't harm us. That would change the course of history. They're ghosts to us, and we'd be ghosts to them. But we'll wake them up a bit."

He reached down into the Woolworth's carrier, and took out a choice pebble.

"Don't, Mike. You're just guessing … you're not being logical … you don't know –"

But it was too late. The pale ghost of the longship came in sight again, with a vision of banked oars moving together. Mike stood up and flung his pebble. He made a whistling noise like a bomb as he watched its flight.

His aim was good, as always. There was a clink and a rattle on wooden boards, and an angry shout. The longship faded away. Mike sat laughing. He picked out two more stones.

"*No*, Mike." They struggled for the tiller. Then came a horrible snarling shout.

The longship was alongside, towering over them, a darker shadow in the fog. They had been seen. There was a swish, Mike yelped, and then something was sticking into *Resurre*'s side. And blood was dripping from Mike's left hand. He stared incredulously, then shouted,

"Bastards, stinking bastards!" and began flinging stones with his right hand for all he was worth. The other boat loomed higher. In a second, they'd be alongside.

Beth grabbed the steering-oar, and pulled. A great random wave rose between the two boats. Then the Vikings were sliding down one side of it, and *Resurre* down the other. One moment, their gunwales had been nearly touching, hands groping out to grab them, and the next minute the two ships were twenty yards apart, and fading away.

Beth kept firm hold of the tiller for the next ten minutes. When she finally brought *Resurre* up into the wind, she sniffed and listened. No sign of Vikings. They were absurd, another daydream. Except that the handkerchief Mike was holding round his hand was red with blood, and a long obscene spear was sticking in the gunwale.

"Let me see your hand, Mike!"

He waved it nonchalantly. "Don't worry. It's nothing." He pulled out the spear. "I like this, though. Genuine Marks and Spencers, Oslo, 700 A.D. It'll go nicely in Uncle Henry's collection. It was worth going for it, wasn't it?"

"No. It could have killed you."

"Oh, bloody hell!" But he was pale, and he let her steer all the way home.

XV

Madeleine pushed away her coffee-cup and said:

"I want you all to pay attention. I've got something important to say."

Mike put his face in his hands and sighed deeply. Madeleine's after-dinner discussions were dreadful. They could go on for hours, especially when people had other things to do.

Having made her announcement, Madeleine, as usual, was in no hurry. She rummaged in her huge handbag for a cigarette, then couldn't find her matches. Once she'd lit up, she put a newspaper on the table and then couldn't find her reading spectacles. Michael went and searched her bedroom for them, with very bad grace.

"I hope this isn't going to take all evening," said Bertrand acidly. "I've still got one of those window-locks to install."

"Don't be such a grump," said Madeleine. "Really, there's no talking to you these days." She put on her reading spectacles, opened the newspaper with a flourish and said, "Now listen carefully, this is important."

"I have never in all my life," said Mike, "known my mother say something was unimportant."

"The more cheap cracks you make," said Madeleine, "the longer this will take."

But just at that moment, she peered out of the window with a frown.

"*Bertrand*. The garden is full of people. Go and see what they want."

There were, in fact, four men, each with a bicycle that he'd laid against the sagging fence. One was the old man who had told Bertrand he wouldn't be able to mend *Resurre*. The other three had the dark dingy look of fishermen. Beth thought they seemed very angry, and yet embarrassed.

"Go and get rid of them," said Madeleine. "They probably want money for something."

Bertrand sighed and got to his feet. Madeleine poured herself another cup of coffee and they all cocked their ears to listen.

The old man was acting as spokesman. His voice was wavery, and his Northumbrian accent strong, so it was hard to tell what he was saying. Beth could see her father, hand against cheek, patiently listening. Then he took his hand away and said sharply:

"Are you trying to tell me how to manage my own property?"

The old man's voice rose, but grew no more coherent.

"As far as I am concerned," said Bertrand, "what my children do with my boat is my business."

The other men were speaking now, stumbling and interrupting each other. You could hear they were very angry indeed.

Bertrand said, "My uncle left me this house and all its contents. Have you legal proof that that boat is *not* part of the contents?"

The old man shouted, "Don't try your townie-talk on us. Your uncle had more sense … He never meant –"

All the men were shouting now. Madeleine got up, her eyes shining with excitement.

"Stay here," she said to the others, and went to join Bertrand. Bertrand was shouting now, which was most unusual.

"I never heard such rubbish in my life. This is the twentieth century, not the tenth. Go away, or I'll call the police."

Beth went to the window and peeped through the curtain. She saw one of the younger men grab Bertrand by the arm. Bertrand tried to shake him off, but the man hung on, bawling into Bertrand's face from a distance of six inches.

Beth saw her father go pale, and felt afraid. Then her father made one sudden violent movement, and the fisherman stumbled back, looking at his hand. He put it under his armpit, as if it hurt.

Beth looked at her father's face. It was a mask of self-disgust. Her father hated using violence; but he couldn't bear people getting too close.

"Get out of my garden! I think you're all completely mad."

The men turned away, and went out of the garden gate. But that was as far as they went. They stood in a group, arguing among themselves and staring at the house.

Bertrand and Madeleine closed the front door and came back into the dining room. Bertrand flung himself down in a chair, and started breathing deeply. Madeleine went to the window and peered past the curtain, giving a running commentary.

"They're still arguing ... one of them's pointing out to sea ..."

"Come away," said Bertrand. "Don't encourage them. They must be the village idiots. Do you know what they wanted? To take *Resurre* away. Said it wasn't fitting that children should use it."

"Why?" said Madeleine, suddenly very interested.

"Oh, they said it was the Wind Eye's Boat or the Dead Boat, or something. The one they used to take the bodies of drowned men off the Farnes, to bury them on Wideopen. They say the monks started it. That would be the House of Farne in the Middle Ages. It can't be the same boat, though. No boat would last that long."

"You mean Uncle Henry used to bury shipwrecked sailors?" said Beth.

"Heavens, no. By Henry's time there'd be the Seahouses Lifeboat. I expect now they use helicopters."

"All this about the Dead Boat sounds pretty authentic to

me," said Madeleine. "You certainly couldn't call it rubbish, Bertrand."

"Oh, I agree with that part of their story. They're the local people – they should know. But then they actually started threatening me with Cuddy. *Saint Cuthbert*, if you please! The way they talked you'd think he was still alive and the village squire. Eiderducks are Cuddy's chickens, stones on the beach are Cuddy's beads. Cuddy's wells, Cuddy's coves – it's unbelievable. They say that if you offend him he can change the wind. They said when the Vikings raided Holy Island, he raised a storm and sank their ships in the harbour, and you can still see the wrecks when the tide's low."

"Oh, my poor darling," said Madeleine, with saccharine sweetness. "But actually, I agree with them."

"You *what*?"

"About the children and the boat, I mean. I don't think they should use it again."

"What possible grounds … ?"

Madeleine picked up the newspaper she'd discarded a quarter of an hour before, and read:

"BAMBURGH MAN PRESUMED DEAD BY DROWNING.

"The Alnwick coroner stated at a resumed inquest last week that Mr Henry Studdard, of Monk's Heugh, Bamburgh, had undoubtedly met his death by drowning. Mr Studdard, aged seventy, was last seen by Alnmouth fisherman Thomas Renwick on the morning of the 10th of February. He was in his sailing-boat off Staple Island. Both vessels hove to, and the two men held a short conversation. Mr Studdard appeared to be in good spirits and, if anything, excited. The sea was calm and the wind light.

"At 6 p.m. the same day, the Seahouses Lifeboat was called out to a boat drifting off Inner Farne. It was found to be empty and towed in to Seahouses harbour, where it was later identified as Mr Studdard's. It was undamaged, and showed no signs of struggle.

"Subsequent searches of the islands and beaches had revealed

no signs of Mr Studdard's body; widespread police enquiries inland had failed to locate his whereabouts. He could therefore be presumed dead. Many bodies, caught in underwater crevices of the Farnes, are never recovered.

"Walter Thomas, coxswain of the Seahouses Lifeboat, said that, in his opinion, Mr Studdard might have been thrown overboard by a freak wave while taking lobsters from his pots. He was a part-time lobster-fisherman, though there were no lobsters in his boat at the time she was found.

"The coroner said that while Studdard had been a keen swimmer in his younger days, he might have been unable to climb back into his boat, once thrown into the water. In a man of Studdard's age there was always the possibility of heart-failure, following the shock of immersion in an icy sea.

"The coroner added a rider condemning the practice of lobster fishing by single-manned boats where the fisherman was of an advanced age. A verdict of Death by Drowning was recorded."

Madeleine looked up triumphantly.

"I knew that boat was a killer! It ought to be burned."

"What paper is that?" asked Bertrand.

"*Alnwick Gazette*, May the twenty-fourth."

"Curiouser and curiouser. I didn't know they'd failed to find the old boy's body. He might still be alive somewhere."

"And pigs might fly," said Madeleine rudely. "Where's he been hiding all this time, then?"

"There's always a chance of amnesia at his age."

"What's kneesia?" asked Sally, thumb in mouth.

"Loss of memory – when you can't remember anything; not even who you are or where you come from." Bertrand looked at his watch. "How's the reception committee outside?"

"Gone," said Madeleine. "For the moment."

"I think I'll go and do some checking-up. The only way of dealing with ignorant yokels like that is to get your facts right. Uncle Henry's solicitor might know a little more than he's said so far."

"And what do we do, if that mob comes back?"

"Good heavens, Madeleine, this is England. They're not the Mafia. Anyway, I'll be back long before it's dark."

"Make sure you are."

Beth stood at the bedroom window, trying to get a breath of air. But the night outside was as still and sultry as the night inside. The noise of the waves on the beach was loud in the stillness. There was still a trace of pale light in the sky to the north, but it just made everywhere else seem darker. She'd be glad when the moon came up.

"Beth," said a restless voice from the other bed, "Beth, can I get a drink of water? My hand hurts. It's *so* hot and itchy."

"Shall I put ointment on it?"

"It doesn't do any good. Can I get a drink?"

"Yes," said Beth snappily. Every nerve in her skin was twitching. It was all this waiting for Bertrand to get back. They had waited and waited. Then, at ten o'clock, a boy had come from the pub at Bamburgh. Bertrand had phoned to say he wouldn't be home till much later; something interesting had come up, and he was driving into Newcastle, to see the director of the Hancock Museum.

"He's got a bee in his bonnet," said Madeleine. "And you know what that means." She had tried to give the boy from the pub a fifty-pence tip for his trouble, but the boy had refused it without saying thank you.

Now it was nearly midnight, and Beth was still at the window, waiting for the first glimpse of the Volvo's headlights. She knew she was wasting her time. Even if Bertrand drove fast, he'd be an hour yet. But she didn't feel like going to bed. She wondered whether she ought to go and ask for one of Madeleine's sleeping-tablets. But she'd always despised the tablets as a sign of weakness. And besides, she didn't want to sleep till Bertrand came.

She stifled a shriek. Something was moving out by the

black shed. It was coming towards the house. She picked up the hand-lamp and shone it. It was Michael. She felt a quite unreasonable rage. He went into the house, and clumped upstairs, and came into her bedroom without knocking. He had a torch in one hand, and a catapult in the other.

"Been scouting. No sign of those prowling bastards."

"But the front door …"

"I've locked it. And checked all the windows. We're as tight as a drum."

"But you must have left the front door unlocked when you went out."

"Oh, yeah. But you had *me* to look after you, then. Besides, they won't come near the house – it's the boat they want. They can just push it down the beach and away."

"We should have locked it up in the shed."

"That wouldn't have stopped them. We'd just have a bust lock as well. Anyway, I don't think they're coming tonight. Tell you what does worry me, though."

"What?"

"Uncle Henry, poor old sod. I bet he didn't just drown. Suppose he sailed back in time to one of the Farnes, and went ashore, and the boat drifted off and left him stuck there. Or maybe the Vikings got him."

"D'you think he knew about *Resurre* being a time-traveller?"

"Stands to reason. That fisherman in the newspaper, the one who last saw him, said he seemed excited."

"Oh, dear. Shouldn't we go and search for him?"

"Through all the years there are? There've been 365,000 days since Cuthbert's time. Multiply that by fifteen islands …"

"Perhaps it's only like Daddy said: amnesia."

"But the police would search all the tramps' hostels. Hey!"

"What?"

"I wonder if Henry had a bald head and a beard. That

dream Sally keeps having, when she sleepwalks – I suppose it couldn't be Henry?"

"Up to his armpits in the sea, singing songs? Out of his mind? A man of seventy wouldn't last very long. If he is alive and not a … Oh, Mike, let's stop talking like this. It makes me feel quite sick."

The bedroom door banged open, making them jump.

But it was only Madeleine in yellow slacks and rollers, looking furious and dragging Sally by the arm.

"You know what I caught this one doing? Playing with the new front-door lock! You're supposed to be in charge of her, Beth. I don't know what Bertrand would say; blast him!

"Anyway, bed, everybody. I want to sleep, even if you don't. If this midnight parliament isn't over in one minute, there's going to be a row from me."

"I'll be awake," whispered Mike. "Just call if you want me."

"Thanks," said Beth.

Beth dozed and wakened a dozen times, to see moonlight streaming through the curtains. Or perhaps she only dreamed she wakened. She felt reality slipping away from her. Was Sally asleep in her own bed, or was she merely dreaming she was?

Then she heard Sally say, in a low glad voice:

"Oh, he's *come*!"

Beth jumped out of bed, feeling sick with relief.

"Who, Daddy? I didn't hear the car!"

"No – the man." Sally was staring out of the window. Beth looked before she thought. If she had thought, she wouldn't have looked.

A figure was standing in the shadow of the black shed, quite motionless. Then it slowly raised its left hand and waved.

"Oh, Mike, help!" As she stood transfixed she heard Mike's hurrying feet. "Mike, it's … here."

"What?"

"That thing … who waves to Sally. By the shed – in the shadow."

Mike turned the powerful beam of the hand-lamp straight on it, and laughed.

"Silly gink. Never noticed that before? It's only a capstan. It's used for hauling *Resurre* out of the sea."

And it was – that peculiar kind of Northumbrian capstan: a revolving post a foot thick and six feet high. What had seemed the figure's eyes were only the holes the rope went through. What had seemed a face was only the gnarled cracks in grey wood, worn for centuries by storms. What had seemed a belted robe was only the rusty iron hoop that stopped the capstan from splitting.

"But it *waved*."

"'Course it waved. *That* waved." Mike made a practised stab with the torch. Somebody had left a marker-buoy leaning against the capstan. As she watched, its tattered rag of a flag waved gently in a stray breath of air.

"God, you women," said Mike, and flicked the torch off.

Immediately, the capstan became a robed figure again. Beth could see sandalled feet, folds in the robe, the whiskered face. She *felt* the eyes watching her. It waved slowly again. Sally waved back. Then she was running down the stairs for the front door.

"Catch her, Mike!" Mike went thundering after her. He caught her undoing the lock, and she started screaming with rage.

"Let me go, Michael! Let me go! He wants to see me!"

Beth heard it all as in a dream, for her eyes were held by the eyes of the figure by the shed.

"Go *away*," she whispered. "You are only a capstan, and a waving flag. You are a trick of the light. You are a figment of my unconscious mind."

The figure shook its head slightly. She reached down in a rage and turned the torch full on it.

It was only a capstan.

Then she couldn't resist switching off.

It was a bearded man. She whimpered, "Please go away."

"What the *hell* is going on!" It was Madeleine, absolutely beside herself with rage.

"There's a man out there. He's trying to get Sally to go out to him."

"By Christ, I know how to deal with *that* sort." Madeleine had her own torch, a long black rubber-covered thing. Now she hefted it like a weapon, and ran downstairs. There was an explosion of rage against Mike, by the front door, and then Madeleine was striding down the garden path in the moonlight. She opened the gate, and began to walk towards the hut and the figure.

Then something quite awful happened.

Madeleine walked up to the figure. And passed it, less than three feet away. Just as she passed it, she paused and peered angrily at the sand-dunes beyond.

She was looking for the intruder there. *She couldn't see the man with the beard.*

But the figure was aware of her. It turned and reached up its waving hand to touch her shoulder.

Just one touch; then Madeleine went on walking towards the sand-dunes. She vanished among them, shining her torch here and there.

Then the figure turned its eyes back on Beth.

"You shan't have Sally," whispered Beth. "You shan't, you shan't."

Then she fainted.

She came round to find Madeleine bending over her.

"What did you go and faint for, you noodle?" said Madeleine. "You had me quite worried for a moment." Her voice was surprisingly warm and kind.

"Where … ?"

"Sally's here … the man's gone. At least *I* couldn't see any sign of him. Nor Mike, here."

"Help me up," said Beth. She made herself look out of the window, at the corner of the black shed. By moonlight; without the torch.

There, in the shadow, stood an old Northumbrian capstan, with a marker-buoy flag waving in the breeze.

The night was empty.

"Yes, he's gone," said Beth.

"Oh, my hand *does* hurt," said Sally.

XVI

Beth was glad to see the sun when she wakened. The tiniest cool breeze was coming through the open window, but she was already sweating.

She felt dead-beat. So it was maddening to have wakened so early; it was only seven. She lay with her eyes shut, listening for reassurance. It came. First the strains of Radio One, floating gently up the corridor. Mike was awake too. In a funny way, the sound of Radio One *was* Mike. He left it playing in his room even when he wasn't there; like a kind of guardian angel. She smiled. Mike made the world all right.

Then there were noises in the kitchen below. Madeleine was pushing last night's washing-up round, rinsing the odd cup here and there, getting enough crockery together for morning tea. She was singing "Goodbye Yellow Brick Road". That was always a good sign. And Sally was with her. She listened to the rhythm of Sally's sharp stabby questions, and Madeleine's longer answers. She couldn't make out a word they were saying, but it was soothing.

"Bap, bap-bap?"

"Dee dee dee dee deedah dee dee, dee-dah."

"Bap, bap-bap?"

Then she remembered Bertrand. Was he home yet? She got up with a groan, and went to the window. The Triumph Spitfire stood alone beside the fence. Bertrand must have stayed overnight in Newcastle.

She looked beyond. Something was different. *Resurre* was there, so the local fishermen hadn't stolen her in the night. Beth caught herself wishing they had; it would make everything a lot simpler.

What was different? And then she realised. There was more sea than usual. The waves seemed to be breaking just beyond the garden fence: big waves. Bertrand would have said it was a spring tide, with the wind behind it.

Why, those waves must be almost up round *Resurre*! As if in answer, she saw the boat's mast suddenly rock. Water was swirling all around her. The waves were lifting her. Beth pulled on a tee-shirt and denims. If she wasn't secured, the boat would be adrift in five minutes.

Then she paused. Wasn't that the best answer anyway? *Resurre* gone and no one to blame? It would end the quarrel with the local men.

Then she realised it went deeper than that. Everything had gone wrong this holiday since Mike found *Resurre*. Oh, it hadn't been a bed of roses before that; but what holiday was, with her family? She could cope with the ordinary problems, the quarrelling. But *Resurre* was dangerous. *Resurre* could short-circuit time itself.

She remembered the horror of sailing into a moonlit night; the invisible thing the seals had watched off Inner Farne; the smell of Vikings. Sally's sleepwalking hadn't started again till they found *Resurre*.

It was all *Resurre*'s fault; *Resurre* had let in the dark. And the dark was getting worse. Every night something came nearer the house …

Of course, they could try and destroy *Resurre*. Burn her. But Beth had an awful feeling it wouldn't be easy. And it might provoke the thing that came in the dark.

But if *Resurre* went of her own accord …

Beth sat on the bed and picked up a pair of binoculars, Michael's binoculars. By the time she'd focussed them, long thin washes of surf were curling round the boat's bow. The sail hadn't been properly lowered, and was flapping like a broken wing. The whole boat seemed to be coming alive.

Then the backwards drag of the waves took her six feet

down the beach, slewing her bows round towards the sea. It was like a bird struggling to escape. Another wave, and her bows were pointing fully seaward. One more and …

And then there was a blue, blurred flicker in the right hand side of the binoculars. She dropped the glasses.

The blue flicker was Sally's dress. She was running through the surf, straight for the boat. She had no shoes on.

Another wave. *Resurre* tipped, and the sail swung viciously at Sally. But Sally dodged, and grabbed the gunwale, and climbed aboard. The next moment, the whole length of *Resurre* was afloat. The half-lowered sail bellied out, and *Resurre* began to move.

"Mike!" screamed Beth, and ran for the stairs.

"Jump, Sally, *jump*! I'll catch you."

Beth gasped as another wave broke in her face. But Sally gave no sign she heard. She was staring in the direction in which *Resurre* was heading. Harkess Rocks.

"Jump!" Beth was already up to her armpits in water and the boat was drifting past. Even with half a sail it was moving faster than Beth could wade.

Sally still didn't stir. Beth was getting left behind. She flung herself forward into a frantic crawl. But too much foam smashed into her face. The boat was drawing away further. And through water-popping ears, Beth could hear the boom of the waves on Harkess Rocks.

She lifted herself up in the water, to see how far away the rocks were. She knew it was a waste of time, but she had to know.

They were very close; ballooning with seaweed and slime.

Then she saw a sight she would never forget to her dying day: Michael running like fury, striped pyjama jacket streaming behind him in the wind, leaping from rock to rock, splashing in puddles, slipping and falling but keeping on.

She trod water to watch. It was Mike or nothing now.

He gave three tremendous kangaroo-hops she'd have thought impossible, and flung himself into the sea in front of *Resurre*.

Resurre began to turn away, out to sea, as if she had a mind of her own. Mike went like a torpedo. Beth saw his arms reach up, very white. His hands caught the gunwale halfway, then slipped off again. With one last despairing grab he caught the sternpost and hung on.

It was enough. *Resurre* hesitated with the additional drag of his body, and came up helplessly into the wind. Now it was Beth's turn to swim fast. Mike was having a terrible job keeping his grip.

With a supreme effort, she made it.

"Up you go," gasped Mike, and gave her a helping heave. Then she pulled him up in turn.

"Sally? You all right?"

Sally sucked her thumb sulkily and said nothing. Next minute the mist came down.

"I can't turn her!"

"Let me try," said Mike.

But it was hopeless. Under the ghastly green light from the horizon, the waves were slate-grey mountains, rippling darkness. It was only bearable while *Resurre* put her bows to them, climbing cleanly. Any attempt to turn her sent her tumbling down sideways, half-filling her with water.

"We'll just have to ride out the storm and hope for the best," said Mike. His pyjamas were transparent with water. A nasty ooze of red blood ran down his shin, from a graze that wouldn't stop bleeding.

But Beth was more worried about Sally. She still hadn't said a word, and she looked at Beth with something like hate. Beth would have liked to wrap her up, but there wasn't a thing except what they were wearing.

"I only hope we can miss the rocks," said Mike, "till we're outside the Farnes."

"Outside the Farnes?" gasped Beth. The thought was terrifying. But Mike flicked his thumb to where a black rock bit up in a burst of creaming spray.

"That's the Megstones. You wouldn't fancy trying to land there?"

"Why can't we control the boat?"

"Maybe it's just the storm. But we seem to be going somewhere, don't we? I mean we're not just sailing round in circles."

"I think we're going to Inner Farne," whispered Beth, trembling. Farne was where the lifeboat had found *Resurre* floating empty. Farne was where the man had first waved to Sally …

"Hey, you don't think …" said Mike.

"*What?*"

"You don't think that it's … Sally controlling the boat? I know it sounds mad, but the look on her face rather matches this storm."

"Don't be daft. She's only a baby."

"Baby nothing. You know when I was trying to get hold of the boat off Harkess Rocks, and slipped? Well, she was kicking at my hands. I didn't tell you, 'cos I didn't want to upset you."

Beth looked at Sally again. Sally stared back as if she hardly knew her.

"That night she went sleepwalking on the beach and nearly drowned. She said she was following the man …"

"She's doing it again," said Mike. "Look."

Beth looked. On the cliffs of Inner Farne, less than a quarter of a mile away, a man was standing.

The water in the channel between Farne and Wide-open should have been calmer, but it wasn't. The Kettle was boiling with foam breaking from concealed rocks.

The man had followed them round the cliffs. Sometimes he would vanish in a dip in the ground, but every time he reappeared he was nearer.

They were almost at the beach of St Cuthbert's Haven. Beth knew the boat would come to land there. And Sally would get off and vanish, like Uncle Henry.

A grim defiance rose in her. *Resurre* was travelling very fast. If, at the vital point opposite the beach, something went amiss, the waves would sweep the boat through the Kettle and out into the open sea.

Now was the time. She turned to the distant figure on the cliff, and summoned up every ounce of rage she could manage.

"Sally is mine. Mine! Mine! Mine!"

The figure on the cliffs grew blurred for a second. It could have been a drift of spray.

Beth shouted, "Mike. Steer for the open sea."

Next minute, all hell broke loose. One of the ropes holding the mast snapped, and the sail came down, beating at their faces. *Resurre* lost her steady rocking-horse rhythm and spun wildly. Water came pouring in over the side.

"We're going aground on Wideopen!" shouted Mike. "I can't hold her."

The whole world was looming rock and spray. The wind seemed full of gleeful screaming voices. Beth thought she could see black goats standing on the rocks amidst the spray. I'm going potty, she thought. I'm seeing things. Then she put her face in her hands and wished she'd never been born. She thought she heard Mike shout, "He's *praying*!" and then everything went black.

"This," said a cheery voice, "is Inner Farne. Half-an-hour here, ladies and gentlemen. Prior Castell's tower is open for inspection, and St Cuthbert's chapel. Please don't cross the barrier ropes, which protect the nesting sites of the terns. Have your landing permits ready, please."

Beth looked up. Mike was sitting in the stern, still in his wet pyjamas, looking pale. The boat was bobbing on a calm sea. A soggy ice-cream wrapper floated past. A bunch of women in headscarves was climbing onto land out of a Seahouses fishing-boat.

Sally was gone.

"Where is she?"

Mike raised his head. "We were just going aground on Wideopen. That bloke on the cliff lifted his arms up and shouted, and the wind turned round. We sort of drifted back towards Farne. That bloke came down to the beach. I couldn't bear to go on looking; I hid in the bottom of the boat. But Sally got all excited. I could feel her jumping up and down and sort of gurgling with delight. Then I heard her jump into the water. I think she made it to the beach. I can't be sure because we were suddenly here." He indicated the trip-boat.

"Oh, Mike!"

"I'm sorry. I couldn't do *anything*."

"Hey, are you kids all right?" It was the skipper of the trip-boat hailing them. "I didn't see you arrive. Have some trouble with your mast?"

"'S okay," mumbled Mike. "We can fix it."

"It's a funny old boat, that," said the skipper. "You kids shouldn't be round here in a boat like that."

"We're just going," said Mike wearily.

Mike mended the rope that held the mast; it had just come unravelled from its mooring. They sailed out to where the skipper of the trip-boat couldn't see them.

"We're going back to get Sally," said Beth. She had a white determined look on her face that reminded Mike of St Joan going to the stake in a movie.

"Do what you like," said Mike. "I'm out of my depth. I'll just sit here."

Beth took firm hold of the steering oar, and willed *Resurre* to go back into the mist. She willed it as she'd never willed anything before in her life. *Resurre* continued her lulling rocking-horse motion over a calm sea strewn with ice-cream wrappers.

An hour later, Mike said softly, "It's no good Beth. You'll just make yourself ill."

"Damn you, damn you, *damn you*!" yelled Beth. "You're just sitting there! You're not even *trying* to help."

"Sorry," said Mike abjectly. "I feel I've had all the stuffing knocked out of me. First that bloke, and then those goats …"

"Goats? You mean, on the rocks of Wideopen? What's so scary about black goats? They probably live wild there."

"Nothing could live on Wideopen. It's just rocks. Besides, they had something on their backs."

"What do you mean, something on their backs?"

Mike gave a sick grin. She had never seen him so crawling and apologetic.

"Oh, nothing. I expect I just imagined it, because I was scared stupid."

"What did you *think* you saw?"

"Little men riding them." He giggled. Horridly. "Take no notice of me."

"I'm not," said Beth in disgust. "Sally's lost, and all you can do is babble about little men riding goats."

"Sorry!"

"If you say sorry again I'll *bit* you. What am I going to tell Daddy about Sally?"

She started to cry, and Mike thought she would never stop. He tried putting an arm round her, but she just shook it off. It was awful. She cried till the tears ran off her chin, till her mouth dribbled saliva; till she hiccuped and finally till she was sick.

Mike took off his pyjama jacket and wiped her face. She was quieter after that, and Mike set a course for the shore.

XVII

"I just don't understand," said Bertrand dully. "I just don't understand how it happened. Perhaps later it will become clear to me. The sea just didn't seem that rough, from the shore. It may be that Sally panicked. Anyway, I think it is true to say you did your best, Beth. And thank you for what you did, Michael. That wound in your leg looks very painful. Madeleine will take you to the doctor's, I'm sure, when she comes back with the police."

Bertrand got up like an old man, pushing with his hands on both arms of his chair. He turned to a pile of big books on the table, opened one, didn't look at it, and closed it again. He opened the front door.

"Shall I come with you?"

"No, Beth. Stay and answer the policeman's questions. I think I'll go for a walk. I want to be alone for a while."

The door closed behind him.

"He thinks she's dead," said Mike.

"I know. But what can we do? She might be dead, for all we know."

"But I don't think she is. I think she made it."

"How can you know, Mike? You were hiding in the bottom of the boat. Besides, even if we told him, you don't think he'd believe us, do you? He'd just say we were suffering from shock. Or mentally unbalanced."

"You mean we'd get a little prick in the arm and a trip to happy-land?"

Beth nodded. "And even if he did believe us, you don't think *Resurre* would go back in time for him, when she wouldn't go back for me? You've got to really believe in *Resurre* before anything happens." She sighed. "But I hate to

98

see him suffering like this."

The police-sergeant was frankly incredulous.

"I still don't get it," he said finally. "It doesn't make sense. Why did she jump out of the boat? Why didn't you see her in the water? She can't have sunk straight away. And St Cuthbert's cove must have been swarming with people. Why didn't you ask for help straight away?"

"The sail fell down," said Mike feebly. "It was so sudden we didn't know what to do."

The police-sergeant walked to the window.

"Is *that* the boat?"

Beth nodded. The police-sergeant started to say something and then stopped. There was a silence.

"If I were you, madam," he said finally to Madeleine, "I'd have that boat locked up straight away, before anything else happens."

Madeleine simply nodded. She didn't look scared or angry, just quiet. Mike couldn't think what had got into her.

"We've got the Seahouses Lifeboat and the Berwick Lifeboat searching now, madam. And I think they're sending a couple of helicopters down from Lossiemouth. We'll leave no stone unturned, I promise you. And I'll come and let you know, the moment I hear ... anything. It could be some time. The Farnes are a funny place. It's sometimes weeks before ... I'll be going then." He picked up his hat and left.

"I'll go and try to find Daddy," said Beth.

"Cup of tea, Mike?" asked Madeleine.

"Yeah." He sat tense in a chair, watching her make it, waiting for the coming storm. Madeleine was always the same. She would start with a pretence of kindness, sympathy, concern. Then her questions would get angrier and angrier. In the end she would be screaming a catalogue of all his faults since he was five years old. She had been known to go on for two hours non-stop, and arguing back only prolonged the agony. It was her way of letting off steam. It was the reason she never got ulcers. The people who lived with her got them instead.

He glanced at her hands holding the teapot; the more they were quivering, the worse the storm would be.

Her hands were perfectly steady.

She gave him his tea, turned away to the sink, and began peeling potatoes. The silence went on and on, with just the noise of the knife on the potatoes.

Scrape, scrape, scrape. It made his stomach churn.

If she didn't start soon, he'd run out of the house screaming.

"We didn't tell that policeman everything, you know!" That should be enough to set her off.

Scrape, scrape, scrape.

"In fact we told him a pack of lies. Deliberately."

She dropped first the knife, and then the potato into the water. Here it came!

But she just mumbled something in a low voice, without turning round.

"What did you say?" His voice sounded very loud and rude in the silence.

"You're trying to make me angry, Mike. Aren't you?"

"Yeah. Suppose so."

"Well it's no use. I can't be angry. I just feel – well, I can't be angry, that's all."

"It must be the shock; about Sally, I mean." But shock had never silenced Madeleine before. The very opposite.

She turned, but he couldn't see her face, because it was against the light of the window.

"No, it's not Sally. It happened last night. When I went out to look for that prowler. I'd have brained him if I'd caught him, I was that angry. And when I got to the black hut, I thought I felt someone touch me, but there was nothing

100

there. Only suddenly I … I felt as if I'd swallowed a whole bottle of tranquillisers."

She laughed feebly. "I once did, you know. After your father died. So I know what it feels like. You go all relaxed down to your little toes, like a baby. Tiny things make you happy, like the smell of the sea and the sound of the waves. Last night I felt like I hadn't felt since I was a kid. I pretended to go on searching down the beach, but I was just enjoying myself really. Then I came back and slept better than I have for years. No sleeping pills either. And this morning my body still feels happy; I keep on wanting to sing. But Sally's drowned. Sally's drowned, and I want to sing."

She dropped into a chair heavily. "Am I going mad, Mike?"

Mike looked at her, his hands tense on the chair-arms with alarm. She *did* look happy. Her eyes were shining, though that could have been tears. There was colour in her cheeks. She looked young and radiant.

Fear made Mike cruel. "You've acted potty for years."

But it didn't needle her. She just said, "I can't get angry. I've been trying all the morning. It's like reaching for the accelerator of a car and finding someone's sawn it off. But Mike, if I can't get angry, I can't *do* anything. I'm helpless. It's anger that kept me going all these years since your father died. *I'd* show the bastards; so many bastards. Do you remember Mr Snaith?"

Mike remembered. Mr Snaith had been his prep-school head. Mr Snaith had caned him unfairly. Madeleine had spent two hours in Mr Snaith's study, and Mr Snaith had emerged like a shaking ghost and apologised to Mike in front of all 3A. Madeleine had been a tigress in defence of her young.

"So many bastards," said Madeleine. "Never any shortage of bastards to get me angry and keep me going. Each day's morning paper was full of them: the I.R.A., wife-battering husbands, corrupt politicians. Anger is so *easy*. It kept me *warm*. Now it's gone. I'm happy but … I'm frightened, Mike." Mike shivered.

"Please *help* me, Mike." Madeleine reached out a hand for him blindly.

Mike jumped up and ran out of the house.

He seemed to wander round the dunes for hours. The sky had turned grey and the wind cold. Everything was pointless.

He wanted to go home to his mother. She would be furious with him and then the slate would be wiped clean … even that awful … *Thing* on the island, that had made him crouch like a baby in the bottom of the boat.

Madeleine's rage was bigger than that … *Thing*. Madeleine's rage was the biggest thing in the whole world.

But not any more. In Madeleine's place, a poor soft mad creature waited at home; so it could plead for his sympathy with creepy fingers.

He'd been afraid for a long time that his mother would go nuts. There'd been times, before, when she sat without speaking for hours, when he heard the surreptitious clink of tablets being taken from bottles in the bathroom. But the tablets had always pulled her round before.

He came back to the black shed and the capstan. The grey rag of the fishing-float waved against the grey sky. He kicked it over in sudden spite.

Then caught his breath.

This was where Madeleine had been standing when she started going nuts. This was where Sally had seen … *him*. And Beth, too.

It all started here.

His mother was not mad. His mother had been got at, by the *Thing* on the island. Nobbled. Knocked out of the fight.

God, it was so unfair. How could anybody ordinary stand up to a thing like that? With its magic cheating tricks!

He began to feel gratifyingly angry. He would get an axe and chop the capstan into little pieces. That would make him feel a lot better. Or he would build a fire round it and burn it. Like they used to burn witches. He began gathering driftwood into a pile. But he had no matches. His matches were in the house.

He walked back to the house, clenching his fists and pretending nothing had happened; it was all a lot of rubbish.

In the kitchen, the radio was on. Some stupid saccharine band was playing "Oh What a Beautiful Morning", and Madeleine was baking cakes and humming to herself. But it was all right. She wasn't crazy, just one of the walking wounded.

"You're not mad," he shouted. "You've been nobbled. Sit down. I can explain everything."

She listened through to the end, without a word, and then got up to take the cakes out of the oven.

"Do you believe me?" he shouted at her. "That there is something out there?"

"I believe you," said Madeleine. "Thousands wouldn't. Thank God you didn't tell Bertrand any of this. He'd have gone up in a blue light."

"What, worse than thinking Sally's dead?"

"Oh, yes. He believes in *death*. A biological necessity. Part of his tidy world. But magic boats and creepies on Farne … I mean, my dear chap, Farne's a *bird-reserve*."

"Oh, come on. Bertrand's a steady enough bloke."

"You haven't lived with him as *I* have. He's steady enough when he can dominate his own little world – where anything he can't smell or measure doesn't exist. Living with Bertrand is like living in a safe dusty little padded cell where you can't even look out of the window. I know there are things in the dark outside; they scare me. But Bertrand is so scared he can't even admit they exist. How's *that* for scared?"

"Mum?"

"Yes?"

"What is it on Farne? Uncle Henry?"

Madeleine gave a pale ghost of her old contemptuous snort, that Mike found very comforting.

"Uncle Henry? *There's* Uncle Henry." She went to the big pile of books on the table and threw a photograph across. It was faded, one corner missing. Uncle Henry had a weak clean-shaven chin, gold-rimmed spectacles and a great flop of silvery hair across his forehead. He bore an eerie resemblance to Bertrand without any of Bertrand's pugnacity.

"Looks like he wouldn't say boo to a goose," said Mike.

"How right you are. Can you imagine him causing trouble, alive *or* dead?"

Mike shook his head. "Then who *is* on Farne?"

Madeleine picked up another book from the table.

"Bertrand brought these back from Newcastle. I've been reading them, while you were sailing the ocean blue in your pyjamas. To soothe my maternal nerves. Read that."

Mike read: *Going into deep water until the swelling waves rose as far as his neck, he spent the dark hours of the night singing praises to the sound of the waves. At daybreak he went up onto the land and began to pray once more, kneeling on the shore. While he was doing this, there came forth from the depths of the sea two creatures commonly called otters. These … began to warm his feet with their breath and sought to dry him with their fur, and when they had finished their ministrations, they received his blessing and slipped away into their native waters …*

Mike drew a deep breath.

"Whew! That's Sally's dream isn't it? The night she went sleepwalking on the beach and nearly drowned. Oh, this is nuts! That was a thousand years ago."

"You're starting to sound like Bertrand. You used *Resurre* to go back to Cuddy's time. Why shouldn't he come to our time?"

"But he's a *saint*! He wouldn't be allowed …"

"What do you know about saints? Old gentlemen in white nightshirts on the Sunday School walls? You only went to Sunday School twice anyway. I've been reading about Cuddy, and he's dangerous. He could control the wind, raise storms. He struck people dead even when he was in his tomb."

"What can we do?"

"Me, nothing. He sent one woman mad just for trespassing in Durham Cathedral graveyard. *I* actually stepped on his tomb. I come out in a cold sweat whenever I think about it. He couldn't stand women near him. I'm thankful he's not done more to me than he has. As it is, I don't dare set foot outside this house. I can't even drive my car: it's an anger car. All I can do is wait for things to happen."

Madeleine put her face in her hands. "Can you imagine what it feels like for *me* to just sit and *wait*?"

The radio went on playing cheerful music. The announcer put in a flip weather-forecast. There was the safe smell of freshly-baked cakes.

"Oh, Mum, this is crazy. This is the twentieth century."

Madeleine looked up. "We're in some kind of deadly game, Mike. We must play by its rules, whether we like it or not."

"Well it – he – hasn't taken *my* rage away. I'm not beaten yet."

"Mike, you haven't got a chance."

Mike paced round the room in a fury.

"There must be something …"

"There's Beth. Maybe Beth could do something. Blessed are the pure in heart, so they say. She's a pious little prig, but she'd die for Sally – or Bertrand. I suppose it's admirable. It's just not me, that's all. I'm going to make the beds now. Someone's got to keep the place tidy."

She stood up.

"Mum?"

"Yes?"

"Why didn't Bertrand spot all this? He's the brightest bloke I know."

"There's none so blind as those who will not see. Actually, there's one nice thing in all this – after three years of Bertrand calling me a silly superstitious, sensation-seeking woman – to find I was right about the supernatural after all!"

"I'm going to read these books."

"Know your enemy, eh? Just remember – Sally chose to go to Farne. She kicked your hands in the boat when you tried to stop her."

"But she's only six!"

"Now you sound like Bertrand again. Didn't you know what you wanted, when you were only six?"

XVIII

Beth shone the torch on the black shed's new padlock.

"We'll never break *that*. Daddy's spent all day putting it on. It's the biggest one I've ever seen."

Mike laughed. "No need. The planks at the back of the shed are rotten: I've pulled half the wall away."

"Oh, Mike, he'll be so angry." Her voice dropped. "I suppose it doesn't matter. It's better than having to watch his face and hearing all those helicopters flying round and round, and knowing everyone's so worried and it's all our fault. But suppose *we* don't come back either?"

"We'll be past worrying, won't we?"

"Oh, don't be so heartless. Poor Daddy. I don't know if we ought to go …"

"You read the books."

"Yes. About how Cuddy sent the storm to drown the Vikings. He seems more like some horrible old wizard than a saint. What did he want Sally *for*? What harm had she done him? She's only a baby. Oh, I could kill him for what he's done, if it was him, if he really exists. Oh, *Mike* … !"

She sat down on the sand and started to cry again.

"If you don't come now," said Mike grimly, "you'll *never* know. They're coming to take *Resurre* away tomorrow."

Beth was still crying as they hauled the boat down to the sea. Mike had to shout at her, to make her keep going, and he was scared Bertrand would hear.

But Bertrand had had a little prick in the arm, and was away in happy-land.

They sailed towards Farne for nearly half an hour. But the mist refused to descend. The lighthouse on Farne mocked them.

"It's not going to work," said Beth in a small voice. "I've wished and wished."

"What are you wishing for?" asked Mike.

"To get back to yesterday, when Sally jumped overboard."

"That's no use. You've had that fight with Cuddy once, and Cuddy won."

"What shall I wish for, then?"

"Have a toffee and think," said Mike. He rustled a bag invitingly in the darkness. Oh, it was good to have Michael there with her in the dark. But she finished the toffee without having a single thought.

Mike said, "Well, look at it from Cuddy's point of view. He's out there somewhere, trying to live like a hermit. I've never heard that hermits were all that gone on having small yappy females around. He's bound to get sick of her. I mean, there'll come a point when he has no further use for her. I mean when he's finished with her. Oh, God, that sounds terrible."

It did sound terrible.

"What I mean," said Mike, trying again, "is if you *wish* to be at the time when he doesn't want her any more –"

The mist came down instantly.

"Why didn't I keep my big mouth shut?" said Mike.

They came out of the mist with a rush, and Beth nearly steered straight into a large rock. Mike took the helm off her, muttering, "Bloody women."

He headed for Farne, nervous as a cat.

Mike raised his binoculars.

"She's there. She's waving. She's jumping up and down." He sounded smug; as if he'd come out top of the class. Was everything a game to him?

Beth could see nothing for tears.

Sad tears, glad tears; she felt like a swamp, a heap.

The boat beached with a bump, throwing her forward onto her knees. Mike helped her out.

"Best of luck."

"Aren't you coming?"

"No. I'll stay and keep an eye on *Resurre*. Don't want her drifting away and stranding the lot of us."

He sounded ashamed and shifty. "You go and get Sally quick, before she bounces over the cliff."

The path seemed as steep as a mountain. Would she never get to the top?

"Hello, Beth. He said you'd come for me, but I was getting a bit worried. I'm *hungry*. Got any chocolate?"

Beth wiped her eyes.

"Sally, you're *filthy*. Look at your hair! How'd you get like that?"

"Well I've been here ten days, and he didn't have any soap. If you think I'm filthy, you ought to have seen him. He ponged worse than Mrs Sullivan's dog."

Beth winced; Mrs Sullivan's dog was a byword throughout Cambridge.

"You all right, Sally?"

"Of course. Only hungry. *Haven't* you got any chocolate?"

"What have you been eating?"

"Old bread and onions. He was awfully fond of onions, but they made my eyes water. He didn't look after himself at all, you know. He was much too busy singing and praying. He even sang in the middle of the night, when he was prowling about. He had to prowl about to keep off the devils. They're *yuk*! Little and spiteful and you can't see their faces, and they ride goats. But they're scared of him, so they live over there."

She pointed to the Wideopens. "I was frightened they'd come and get me after he'd gone, but I think he fixed them till you came."

"Where is he?"

"Oh, he's gone. A sort of king came and took him away. He

109

argued and argued, but they still took him. He was crying; he didn't want to go."

"You mean they arrested him?"

"Oh, no. They dressed him up in beautiful clothes, with this sort of crown hat. But he still didn't want to go. He threw his golden cloak down on the grass, but he had to go in the end. He was *awfully* sad."

"What did you do all the time?"

"We went for walks. Do you know, he dropped his book over the cliff into the sea once, and a seal brought it back to him in its mouth! The seals were always watching him. I threw the book back in the sea to see if the seal would fetch it again, but then he got cross with me.

"And once we saw two ravens stealing straw from the roof of his hut, to build their nest. He shouted at them like anything, and sent them away. But afterwards one came back and walked up to him dragging its wings, like saying it was sorry. Then he let them come back again. He's awfully good with birds and animals."

"What kind of things did he say to them?"

"Don't know. It was all double-Dutch. He talked to me by signs – we got quite good at it."

Beth stared about her. She saw the circular building, which Bertrand had called a sheepfold.

"Is that his house?"

"Yes, but we mustn't go there. He never let me go inside, but he took that king in. I don't think he likes me being near his things. But he carried me on his shoulders. It was a bit like riding a horse, because his robe and beard were all prickly."

She glanced round nervously.

"We'd better go, Beth. The devils might come. They're always trying to creep back. They used to live here once, I think, but he drove them out."

They walked back towards *Resurre*. Then Sally stopped and turned.

"I better tell you one thing. One day we were both very hungry. I was even eating onions. He pointed to a big bird that was flying out at sea, and made eating signs. I thought he was going to kill the bird and eat it, and I was sad because it was a beautiful bird. But then it came flying in with a huge fish in its claws, and dropped it on a rock. He told me to go and fetch it. I knew I couldn't manage, 'cos of my bad hand, and the fish was so big. But *he* knows everything, and can do anything and – well you just don't argue with him. So I went and tried, and I managed. And then he sent me back with half the fish for the bird, 'cos it was waiting for its dinner. And it wasn't till I got back that I noticed –" Sally held out her good hand.

"Noticed what?" said Beth.

Sally blushed and waggled the hand. Then Beth gasped. Sally was not holding out her good right hand. She was holding out her bad left hand. The glove was off it, and it was as pink and perfect as the other.

Beth's head spun. Sally went gabbling on.

"The worst part was going to the loo. It's that box built out right over the sea, and just a plank to sit on. When it was stormy I kept looking down at the waves, and I got so dizzy I nearly fell ..."

But Beth wasn't listening.

XIX

Farne slipped astern. Mike, at the steering-oar, had caught the wind just right; the sharp bow began to sing its chuckling song. Mike sighed with relief. He groped for the bag of toffees and threw it to Sally who attacked it ravenously. When she had four in her mouth at once, she said:

"Michael, what's a wind eye?"

Mike glanced at Beth, and then said, "Why do you ask that, Sally?"

"*He* talked about it, to himself. It was about the only words he said that I could understand."

"Well," said Mike cautiously, "those fishermen said this was the Wind Eye's boat."

"But what *is* a wind eye?"

Mike shrugged. "Your guess is as good as mine. Old sailors used to talk about being in the eye of the wind, and then there's the eye of a hurricane, which is the calm patch in the middle of a cyclone. But we don't get hurricanes round here."

"I know *that*!" said Sally, unwrapping a fifth toffee.

"I did wonder … Remember the time we sailed to Farne in the dark, and the dawn came up? Remember the thing the seals were watching? The ripples on the water with nothing to make them? That caught up the boat and drove us up to Holy Island? Perhaps that was a Wind Eye."

"Ooh, a sort of sea-monster," said Sally.

"For heaven's sake, Mike," Beth exploded. "Aren't we in enough trouble, without you dreaming up more mysteries?"

"What you mean, enough trouble? We'll be home in half-an-hour. All's well that ends well. We can stick *Resurre* back in the shed, nail the planks back, shove Sally into bed, and no one the wiser. There she'll be in the morning, surprise, surprise."

"Oh, Mike! How can you be such an idiot? We can't do that."

"Why not?" asked Mike. "It's broad daylight here, but it's the middle of the night back home. I've got some fresh nails, and I can hammer quietly."

"But there's the police."

"Sally can lose her memory. Can't you, Sally? God bless amnesia."

"Have I got kneesia?" asked Sally with interest.

"You're going to have, love, when I've finished with you. We can wangle the lot, Beth. My mum's on our side now, remember. We can wash Sally's hair in the kitchen."

"What about that awful dress?"

"Burn it. She's got one nearly like it."

"But what about … her hand?"

"Shove another glove on it and pretend there's no change."

"It won't work, Mike."

"All right – think of something better, if you're so clever."

"I can't."

"Well, then. Look. The longer we can hold off being rumbled, the better. If we can get back to Cambridge, it'll be a nine day's wonder. Just one of those things. A great unsolved mystery of the sea, like the *Marie Celeste*."

"We can try," said Beth. But her heart wasn't in it. Mike didn't know Bertrand …

The doctor looked up, puzzled.

"There's nothing wrong with this hand. Is this some kind of joke?"

"You could say that," said Bertrand, and laughed. Beth wished he'd stop laughing like that.

The doctor stirred uncomfortably. He played with a paper-knife marked *Dettol* and looked sideways at Bertrand.

"Identical twins?"

"There is no twin-sister. This is the same girl you saw on Tuesday. Only the hand is different."

The doctor looked at Beth. Beth nodded wearily. It was six hours since Sally had picked up the salt-cellar with the wrong hand. It felt like six years.

"I'd like your *scientific* opinion, doctor," said Bertrand. He picked up Sally's hand as if it was something obscene, and waggled it under the doctor's nose. Sally began crying again.

"Let's take the little girl outside," said the doctor. "My receptionist can see to her."

"She'll stay here!" said Bertrand. "I want them to hear all you have to say. Your *scientific* opinion, doctor, please."

The doctor shrugged. "I haven't got one. On Tuesday that hand was crippled with third-degree burns. Today it's perfect. Call it a miracle, if you like. These things happen to every doctor, sooner or later. I had to tell one old man he was dying of cancer. A year later he walked in hale and well. No trace of cancer. You get used to it, eventually. You don't think about it any more."

"Are you a doctor," sneered Bertrand, "or a Catholic priest? You'll be asking next if we've been on a day-trip to Lourdes."

The doctor flushed; but he stayed frighteningly calm.

"I'm not even a Christian. But I am a doctor. And I tell you, as a doctor, that if you go on like this, you'll not only have a sick child on your hands, but you'll be a very sick man yourself. Meanwhile, I have a full surgery, and it's not part of my National Health duties to sit here and be insulted. Do you want something to calm your nerves?"

"Go to hell!" shouted Bertrand, and pulled Sally out of the room so violently that her knees gave way in the doorway.

She began screaming hysterically in the waiting-room.

"What can I do?" asked Beth.

"Keep the child away from him. And give him these, if he'll take them." The doctor wrote a prescription and put it in her hand. "You can ring me day or night, if you think I can help. Here's my phone-number."

His kindness made Beth even more afraid.

"Is my father going ... mad?"

"Not with anything in the textbooks."

"He's an atheist, you see."

The doctor smiled briefly. "Yes, I'd gathered that."

"It's ... Cuddy."

Beth wondered if the doctor would think she was going mad too. But he just smiled again and said, "Yes ... I've heard things."

Outside in the Volvo, Sally was huddled in the back seat, still sobbing. Bertrand's hands were tight on the steering-wheel. Beth got in.

"Daddy?"

Bertrand went on staring straight ahead at a lamp-post. "Yes?"

"We've got Sally back, and she's not a cripple any more. She won't feel different from other children. You must admit that's good."

"Good? The mercy of God? Why *Sally*? Why does Sally deserve mercy, more than all the Vietnamese Sallys who got frizzled up with napalm? Or the English Sallys who die of leukaemia every year? Is there some kind of heavenly football-pool?"

"I don't know."

He turned and looked at her as if she was an enemy.

"Well, you should know. You're the Christian. I allowed you to be a Christian. I thought if I left you alone, you'd grow out of it in time. But now, it seems, you're right and I'm wrong."

"We didn't want to tell you. We knew it would upset you. That's why Mike lied. That's why Sally wouldn't say anything. We didn't want to hurt you."

"So I'm a child now, am I? To have things hidden from me."

"Why are you so bitter?"

"Because Sally's hand is being used as bait to catch me. Once I acknowledge it's a miracle, the Church can move in and do a takeover. The Pope who let six million Jews be gassed, and never lifted a finger. Catholic nuns who starve orphan children, and lock them in cupboards and beat them till they bleed. No birth-control in a world that's destroying itself through over-population. The Inquisition. Need I go on? That's the reason behind Sally's hand. It's not love – it's power-politics!"

"I'm sorry."

"Is that all you can say?"

She touched his arm, but he threw her off, put the car in gear and shot off up Bailiffgate, missing a bus by inches. Driving worse than Madeleine.

Beth gave a jump.

"What's the matter?" asked Madeleine.

"I thought I heard Sally crying."

Madeleine shook her head. "I was up five minutes ago. She's fast asleep. I gave her a sleeping-tablet."

Beth went to the window and drew back the curtain. There was moonlight outside. No sign of Bertrand.

"I wonder what Daddy's doing?"

"Oh, forget him," said Mike. "Let's have an hour's peace."

"I'm sorry I had to speak to him like that," said Madeleine, and for once she *did* sound sorry. "But I had to get him to leave Sally alone."

"Oh, you were right," said Beth. "But now he thinks we're all against him. He must be awfully lonely out in the dark."

116

"Now we've got *two* men lurking out there," said Mike, and laughed mirthlessly.

"Shut up, Mike," said Madeleine.

"Suit yourself." He buried himself again in the Cuthbert book. The tick of the clock was loud, and the fall of hot cinders in the grate. The night was really much too warm for a fire, but the flames helped somehow.

"Hey," said Mike. "Listen to this. This is something else Sally talked about." He put on his drony reading voice:

"The saint saw two ravens tearing to pieces the roof of his shelter and making for themselves a nest. He bade them, with a slight motion of his hand, not to do this. But when they disregarded him, at last his spirit was moved and sternly bidding them to depart in the name of Jesus Christ, he banished them.

"But after three days, one returned to the feet of the man of God as he was digging in the ground, and, settling above the furrow with outspread wings and drooped head, began to croak loudly for pardon. Recognising their penitence, he gave them permission to return. Those ravens returned to the island with a little gift. For each held in his beak a piece of swine's lard which it placed before his feet. Most trustworthy witnesses, who for a whole year greased their boots with this lard, told me of these things ..." Mike sniggered. "That's what I call a practical apology: Anglo-Saxon boot-polish!"

"I wish you'd give over with that book," said Madeleine. "If there's one thing we don't need, it's documentary evidence that Cuthbert was, is, and forever will be out there. I had to listen for an hour while Bertrand talked about *real* time, and *apparent* time, and *presumptive* time and *absolute* time and time flowing not in a straight line but in loops, and *Resurre* crossing from one loop to another. In the end I couldn't remember which day of the week it was."

"You're thick, like all women," said Mike without looking up. "It says here that Cuthbert built a loo over Cuthbert's Gut, like Sally said, too. Must have been bloody draughty."

But Madeleine was not to be provoked.

"I'll go and heat a can of soup. It will do us all a bit of good."

"Haha!" said Mike, still deep in the book. "Here's a bit to make your flesh creep, Beth. About Wideopen.

"Here demons are believed to reside, who were compelled by St Cuthbert to quit his island ... the brethren have seen them all of a sudden, clad in cowls and riding upon goats, black in complexion, short in stature, their countenances most hideous, their heads long, the appearance of the whole troop horrible ... like soldiers they brandished in their hands lances, which they darted after the fashion of war. At first the Sign of the Cross was sufficient to repel their attacks ..."

"You're making that up."

"I'm not, honest. Look, it's here. By our local correspondent, Bartholomew the Hermit."

"Uurgh," said Beth. "Stop making things worse. You're laughing now, but you didn't laugh when you thought *you* saw them."

"Let's find some more gruey bits!"

"Mike?"

"Yeah?"

"What d'you think's the matter with Bertrand, really?"

"He's trying to decide how to get his own back on Cuddy. You know how he can't stand being proved wrong. Don't you remember that time the Oxford bloke attacked him in the *Observer*? He was just like this – until he'd written that book to prove the bloke wrong. He's O.K., Bertrand – till somebody stubs him out, and then he turns into a bloody sadistic maniac."

"You're unfair. And horrible." Beth's eyes filled with tears. "I'm going out to find him."

She hadn't far to look. He was sitting in *Resurre*, hand on cheek, so still he made her jump.

"Daddy?"

He came back to life from a long way off.

"I've been a fool, Beth."

"You mean … everything's all right?"

But Bertrand's voice was too bitter for any apology.

"I mean I've had my eyes shut too long; believed in scientists who had closed minds. Oh, others have hinted more. Geller bending his spoons on television, or that fellow Watson with his book *Supernature*. But all of them such flashy specious people. I thought they were charlatans."

"And now?"

"Supernature exists. That creature – Cuddy – proved it with Sally's hand. I can see the whole pattern now. Cuthbert was one of the Celtic missionary saints, all said to have power over winds, waves, plants and animals. They must have grasped the essence of Supernature a thousand years before Watson coined the word. How, I don't yet know. All that meditation and fasting may have cleared their minds of prejudice and preconceptions. And I've been such a blind *idiot*."

"But you aren't a scientist."

"That's no excuse," said Bertrand pettishly. "But all this has nothing to do with Christianity, you know. It will all be explained by science, once scientists open their eyes."

"Even the devils on Wideopen?"

"Devils? Poppycock! That's the sort of thing the Church tagged on later. D'you think the Church wanted the common people sharing its new knowledge? They wrapped it up in mumbo-jumbo about devils and angels and all the rest of it. Salvation. Transubstantiation. Obfuscation. All of it. Now we've got to strip off the mumbo-jumbo, and experiment. Develop Supernature for everyone's good – not just for a few religious cranks."

"Oh!" It was a very cold disapproving "oh", but she couldn't stop it. Bertrand chuckled in his new nasty way.

"Scared, Beth? For your precious Cuddy and your precious

Church and your precious Heaven? Scared it might all prove explicable by science after all?"

"What are you going to do?"

"I'm going to try an experiment on your Cuddy. First I intend to find out whether he did sink those Viking longships off Holy Island, as the fishermen say. I can hire skin-diving gear in Newcastle."

"And if he did?"

"I'm going to sail *Resurre* back to the morning of the raid – and the great storm."

"What *for*? You'll be drowned."

"Call it a moral protest. Remember the French plan for atomic tests in the Pacific? Remember how those Australian yachtsmen sailed their boats into the test area so the French couldn't explode their bomb? Well, I'll do the same to Cuddy's storm."

"But he won't know you're there!"

"Your precious Cuddy knows everything that happens to *Resurre*. He knew what was in Sally's mind – so I assume he knows what's in mine."

"But …"

"And then he'll have a choice, won't he? He can either hold back his storm, or drown an innocent man who's working for peace."

"What do you mean, working for peace?"

"Well, I can warn the monks, so they escape in time. Or try reasoning with the Vikings. Did anyone ever try *reasoning* with the Vikings?"

"You can't speak their language."

"Cuddy managed Sally with sign-language. What he can do, I can do."

"You hate him, don't you? You want to stub him out, because he healed Sally's hand that you burnt. It's just like Mike says."

"Oh, Michael says that, does he?" There was a very sharp

120

edge in Bertrand's voice now. "Well, perhaps Michael is right. I didn't ask Cuddy to interfere with my life. He chose to. So why shouldn't I interfere with his? Maybe he's had his own creepy little way a bit too long."

"You're mad. Madeleine said —" Beth sealed her lips together, but it was too late.

"Oho! Madeleine too? What a nice family I have. Well, since you all love me so much, you can't really object if I get myself drowned. Not that I intend to. There are too many secrets to discover."

"Oh, Daddy!" Beth fought back terror and tears. "*Resurre* won't obey you."

"Then no harm can come to me."

"Can I come with you?"

"You can come when I go skin-diving. I'll need some help with the oxygen cylinders."

"All right." She couldn't fight any more.

"Poor old Beth." Bertrand's voice had a pitying kindness she couldn't bear.

It felt as if they were flying, except for the wet hiss of the Volvo's tyres. The sky was pale and huge, and reflected endlessly in the wet sand all the way to Holy Island. Clouds of feeding seabirds rose ahead of their bonnet, circled and landed further off. Every so often they drove through a puddle, and the water drummed on the underside of the car.

"We'll be there in five minutes," said Bertrand. "It'll be a long search, I expect. I'll drop marker-buoys, and surface every twenty minutes. If anyone enquires, say I'm doing a marine-life survey."

They parked as near the sea-edge as possible. Bertrand got into his wet-suit. His hands were swift and sure; the old Bertrand had returned. In a funny frail way, Beth was almost happy.

"Take care … please."

"You know me, old Slow and Sure." He put on his face-mask and tested the air-supply.

Beth looked up towards the village. Two children came out of a cottage door, stared for a minute, and went back inside. Then their mother came out, drying her hands on her apron. She stared longer, then went off up the village street, almost running.

"Cheeroh, then," boomed Bertrand. His face behind the mask was already distant and unreadable. He flip-flopped through the shallows. The flat blue water swallowed up his black figure, first to the waist and then completely. Beth felt suddenly lonely.

The woman from the cottage was back. She had the old man with the bicycle with her. The old man sent her home, and walked down towards Beth.

"What's your father doing, hinny?"

"Examining the marine-life." Fear made her voice come out cold and haughty; but he went on staring at her until she had to drop her eyes.

"Ye're lying, hinny. He's meddling with what doesn't consarn him. Again."

"He's not harming anybody."

"That's for us to decide. It's oor island."

"It's not. The seashore is Crown Property. It belongs to the government. *Anyone* can use it."

"We'll see," said the old man. "Ah've rung for the poliss."

They stood in silence for a very long time. The old man kept playing with the brakes of his bicycle. They made a tiny rusty screech that made Beth want to scream.

Other men came drifting down from the village; from streets with names so old they no longer made sense; Prior Rawe, Baggot Heugh and Cuddy's Walls. Any woman who tried to join them, they sent home again. The children were sent home too. The men stopped in groups, twenty or thirty feet away. They were laughing and excited, like men before some football game; but when Beth looked at them, they turned their eyes away. And they were slowly drifting forward, until they formed a circle round Beth.

"What's your father after, hinny?" asked the old man again.

"He's looking for the remains of the Viking-ships." Somehow, Beth found it impossible to lie this time.

"Aye," said the old man, as if he'd known all along. "He's a wrong 'un, your dad. No respect. Not like the last one. *He* knew his place."

"What last one?" asked Beth. But the old man just shook his head and wouldn't answer.

There was a sudden loud scrunching that made Beth jump. But it was only a Panda-car, coming down the beach. The nice police-sergeant got out, looking worried.

"Morning, Mr Milburn," he said to the old man. His voice was very respectful. Almost cringing, Beth thought.

"Morning, sergeant. Ah'll just tek a walk, while you explain things to this lass here." He wheeled his bike through the waiting crowd.

The sergeant took off his cap, and wiped his sweating brow.

"This won't do, miss. This won't do at all. You'll have to move on. How long has your father been down?"

Beth looked at her watch. She saw with disgust that her hand was shaking.

"He'll be up in five minutes."

"That will do, if you go then. I'll just wait and see you safe away."

"We aren't breaking the law, are we?"

"Well, no, miss. Not exactly. But there's law and law, if you see what I mean. Law's not quite the same on Holy Island."

"Why?"

"Well, I'm in charge of Holy Island, see, miss. But I don't

123

live here. The first policeman they ever had, years ago, he lived here. But then he was born on the Island. They accepted him. But when he retired, they wouldn't let a new policeman live here. And we haven't lived here since."

"But how can they stop you?"

"Oh, easy. Not serving the policeman's wife in the village shops. Not talking to her, or him. Doesn't sound much, but it works. People here are a law unto themselves. It's living on an island, cut off. Oh, they're not a bad lot, if you leave 'em be; just a bit strange like. They've mostly been here since –"

The crowd stirred.

"Morning, sergeant," boomed Bertrand. "Give me that other cylinder, Beth, will you? Clip it on my back."

"You'll have to go, sir. I've had a complaint. The local people don't like what you're doing."

"Then they can lump it," said Bertrand. "I'm not breaking the law."

"There may be a breach of the peace if you stay, sir!"

Bertrand looked at the circle of fishermen; his lip curled ever so slightly.

"It won't be me that breaches the peace first." Bertrand tested his air again, and flip-flopped back into the sea. The old man came back.

"Wouldn't listen, would he?"

"I did my best, Mr Milburn."

"Aye, well," said the old man. "Thank you for the effort. We try and keep inside the law, here. You'll be wanting to get away, I expect. You've got a busy job."

"No fighting, Mr Milburn!"

The old man turned his back. The sergeant looked at Beth pleadingly.

"Try and persuade your father, miss. There's nothing else I can do. These fishermen haven't done anything illegal, and they won't while I'm here. But I'm due in Alnmouth at twelve."

124

"Goodbye, sergeant," said the old man. The Panda drove off in a shower of pebbles. The fishermen moved in closer. Beth stared at them defiantly. They looked decent ordinary men, but they were full of some excitement that made it hard for Beth to breathe. Men – they looked more like a pack of dogs she'd once seen, just before they killed a cat. It seemed a lot more than twenty minutes before Bertrand came splashing out of the water again.

"Still here?" he said to the old man. "I wonder you people ever catch any fish at all." He turned to Beth.

"Give me that last cylinder. I think I'm on to something."

The old man reached up and tried to snatch the mask off Bertrand's head. Bertrand seemed to push him away gently enough, but the old man got tangled up in his bike and fell down.

There was an ugly sound from the crowd. Several fishermen hauled the old man to his feet, and tried to wipe the wet sand off him. One turned and aimed a wild blow at Bertrand. Bertrand moved his head ever so slightly, and the blow missed.

"If you want to brawl, kindly allow me to take off this equipment first. It doesn't belong to me. And how many am I going to have to fight at once? Three? Five?"

Bertrand's voice was slow and cool, but he was quivering; the little drops of water on his wet-suit shook. The fishermen noticed, and nudged each other, with a gloating look on their faces. They thought he was afraid.

"Hughie," shouted the fishermen. "Big Hughie!" They were pushing someone forward from the back of the crowd.

Big Hughie was huge; his fisherman's smock would have fitted a rhinoceros. His hair was cropped, and from the scars on his face, he'd been in fights before. There were steel plates on his boots, and he looked as if he enjoyed hurting people.

Bertrand took off his equipment, but kept on his wet-suit.

He glistened like a seal. He placed his feet a little way apart, kept his hands by his side and began to breathe deeply. Then he looked Hughie straight in the face and said, quite distinctly:

"Animal!"

Quick as a flash, Hughie aimed a kick at Bertrand's stomach. But Bertrand simply swayed six inches to one side and Hughie went down on his back like a stranded whale.

"I must make it clear," said Bertrand, "that this fight was not of my making, and I will not be held responsible for any resulting damage. I haven't hurt him – yet."

Hughie got to his feet in an ominous way.

"Smash him, Hughie!" shouted a man, and there was a growl of agreement from the crowd.

Beth felt sick. The men were awful, but her father was worse. Her father knew exactly what he was doing; uttering reasonable words but using them as goads and whips to inflame the fishermen's anger. If it got into a police-court, the fishermen would be found guilty; and cowardly. Thirty men against one. But it was Bertrand who was making the fight; by the curl of his lip, by the arrogant way he stood with his hands on his hips.

Bertrand *wanted* to fight; using the skills he had gained over twenty years of Judo-training, skills the men could never understand, let alone equal. She recalled with pain her father saying that Judo was invented by peaceful Buddhist monks, as a last resort against men of blind violence who couldn't be reasoned with. Who was the man of violence now?

"Stop!" Beth wasn't the only one who had seen this. The old man had put a hand on Hughie's arm. "Stop it, Hughie!"

"Animal!" said Bertrand to Hughie again.

"Stop, Hughie. Think of your bairns. Who'll work the boat if he breks your arm?"

Warring emotions played across Hughie's heavy face. The

old man stroked his arm, as one might soothe a frightened animal.

"Do as aah telt ye, Hughie. Ye're too good to mek sport for the likes of him."

"Aaargh," said Hughie in despair of understanding. But he turned and walked away.

"I'm glad he's seen sense," said Bertrand. He wiped his hands on his wet-suit, as if he'd touched something dirty.

The old man took something from his pocket and threw it on the sand. Even Beth could tell it was a Viking sword-hilt. Other men threw down other objects; two bronze spearheads, wrist-ornaments.

"Tek them. Tek them and leave us be. Tek them back to your bliddy posh college and put them in a glass case and write your bliddy rubbish about them."

The old man turned to the other men. "Leave him be, lads. He's oot of our hands now. Leave him to the Wind Eye."

They all trailed off.

Beth stared about her. What *was* the Wind Eye? The wind was everywhere. Who could escape the wind?

Bertrand stood staring at the evidence he'd sought.

"They must have trawled these things up in their nets. Sheer ignorance, keeping valuable finds like that, holding up research."

Beth pitied him, more than if he'd lost the fight.

XX

"Here's Madeleine," said Beth. "She's coming."

They all looked up from the water's edge. Monk's Heugh door was opening. Madeleine was walking towards them across the sand. She walked hesitantly, like someone who has been ill. She kept on glancing nervously at the sky. It was brave and pathetic, and horribly embarrassing.

She didn't look at Beth and Mike. She looked at Bertrand standing ready by *Resurre*.

"I'm *pleading* with you," said Madeleine. "I never pleaded with you before. Doesn't that make any difference?"

"Sorry, no," said Bertrand. He steadied *Resurre* with one foot on the gunwale. Five minutes more and the tide would take her.

"I never thought you'd change your mind for *me*," said Madeleine. "But what about your kids? What'll they do, when you don't come back?"

"They'll manage. There's fifty thousand life-insurance."

"Money!" Madeleine made it sound unclean. "They don't need money. They need *you*, you silly oaf!" Were there tears in her eyes?

"Please don't make a scene," said Bertrand. "This is only a scientific experiment. I could be home by tea-time."

Just for a second, Madeleine's eyes sparked the old anger. Then she looked towards Farne, and was calm again. "Remember what you said to me in Durham Cathedral, Bertrand? Just before I stepped on the tomb? Now I'll say it to you. Don't make a fool of yourself, Bertrand. If you do come back, you'll find me with Sally."

She walked back to the house with great dignity.

Beth looked at her father in his blue fisherman's smock,

jeans and sandals. With his long hair blowing in the breeze, eyes bright, he might have been a Saxon thegn going to war. She knew he wasn't coming back.

Bertrand's face softened slightly.

"Don't fret, Beth. Remember Socrates; to a good man no evil thing can happen."

But Beth remembered the way her father had dragged Sally screaming from the doctor's surgery. How he had goaded Big Hughie on Holy Island. She no longer believed her father was a good man. But she still loved him.

"I'm going in the cause of peace, Beth."

Fool, she thought, fool. But she only said, "Let me go with you."

"No. Certainly not. You must stay and help Madeleine. Give my love to Sally. Where is she, by the way?"

"*By the way*?" shouted Beth. "*By the way* she just happens to be breaking her heart in her bedroom."

"Don't hate me, Beth. If I stayed with you all, I think I'd go mad. I have to know, you see."

"Know what? That you're cleverer than a saint? Cleverer than Cuddy? You're not, anyway."

"Let's not quarrel now. I'm off. Cheeroh, Michael!"

Mike just stared at him.

There came an extra-high wave; Bertrand judged it beautifully, and before Beth could move, he was seaborne and raising the sail.

He waved once, then *Resurre* faded into the mist.

"Oh God," said Beth dully. "What can I do? What can I do?" She went on standing there, repeating herself like a stuck gramophone record, while the tide washed further and further in round her wellingtons.

Behind her, Michael was frantic. Beth seemed to be falling apart like a beloved book left out in the rain. And there was nothing he could do. And if he could do nothing, he *was* nothing. Always before, no matter how bad things had been, there'd been a way to help her, by arguing or lying or fighting. But now …

He began picking sticks and stones off the beach and hurling them at the hated sea, the mist where *Resurre* had vanished. He could hear an endless stream of swear-words pouring out of his own mouth, to be lost in the sound of the waves.

Then he looked down and saw.

For some reason, Bertrand hadn't bothered to take *Resurre*'s steering oar.

"Beth, look!" She turned without seeing. He had to push the oar into her hands. "It's part of *Resurre*. Perhaps it will take us if we swim with it."

"Where? We'll never catch up with Daddy. He'll never come back; he'll never change his mind for me. He wouldn't before; he couldn't *bear* to …"

"It might take us … to … to Cuddy …"

It was unthinkable, facing that spectral horror again. But it was better than watching Beth fall apart like this.

"O.K.," said Beth, and began to walk straight into the waves, carrying the steering-oar. He had to pull her back.

"You're wearing too much. Your wellies will drag you down."

She took off her wellingtons, her trousers and sweater, and dropped them in the water. The waves took them, soaked them black, and tumbled them away. Beth stood up in her bra and pants, looking thin and goosepimply, and turning blue. Michael kicked off most of his own clothes and they waded out through the surf, carrying the oar.

As their feet left the sand and they started swimming, the mist closed down. At first the water was warmer than the air. Then it went so cold it made Mike gasp.

At the same moment the mist cleared. Their sunny morning was gone. To the east, clouds banked high and leaden. The hump of Farne shone pale against them, lit by westering sunlight. There was no white patch and no lighthouse. Mike's heart leapt; his plan had worked.

Farne was nothing like three miles off; the oar must have jumped in space as well as time. But there was an uneven choppy swell that slapped water in their faces, no matter how hard they tried to judge it. They began to swallow a lot of water. Mike could hear Beth gasping. Best not to look at the island too often, or they'd get discouraged.

When he did look, it was closer than he'd dared hope. The oar was helping them, as *Resurre* had always done.

But not fast enough for Beth. She turned a white hair-streaked face and shouted, "Stop holding us back!"

"I'm not!" But deep down inside, he knew he was. He did not want to face … Cuddy.

But still the island crags drew nearer. Suddenly they were too near.

"More south," shouted Beth. "We'll have to go round the Stack to get to the Haven. We can't land here."

Miserably Mike tried willing himself round the Stack. His mind refused. If they reached the Haven they'd have to land and …

"Sorry. I tried. I can't."

"Let go the oar then!"

"I daren't. I'll drown. I can't make it back to the beach without the oar. We'll have to turn back."

"I will *not*. Try again!"

But all they did was to get trapped in the gully west of the Stack, where the water circled thick with brown foam and driftwood, and underwater rocks felt cruelly for their flailing feet.

"Jump ashore," shouted Beth.

Blindly obedient, he grabbed for a ledge. As his fingers found one, a wave lifted him and threw him down again, breaking his hold. He blew water out of his nose and mouth, and saw Beth crouched on a tiny ledge four feet above him. She looked down, and pointed out to sea.

"Go home, Michael. Go home!"

"No." It came out as a groan. Then another wave picked him up and banged him down, turning his right knee into a lump of pure agony.

He let the rebounding wave take him. Somewhere in the middle of its white blindness, his hand grasped the oar. By the time he got his head above water, and cleared his eyes and ears, the island was fifty yards astern. Beth was only a thin patch of pink at the bottom of a vertical black cliff. She waved once then turned her head away.

He knew she could never climb the Stack; not with bare feet. She would cling on for a bit. Then, as her hands got numb, she would fall off and drown. But there was nothing he could do about it now. There was nothing he could do about anything. He was a failure.

He'd always thought that if he was tough enough, and clever enough, he could get away with anything. But his toughness, faced with Cuddy, had crumpled like limp lettuce. And his cleverness had only succeeded in getting Beth killed. Beth, the only person he really cared about.

Beth was going to die. Bertrand was going to die. Madeleine was a shattered wreck, terrified to leave the house.

God, what a mess. How did you arrange funerals for people dead in another time? What would the police say? How would the family get back to Cambridge if Madeleine couldn't drive the car? How did you stop little kids crying?

He loathed misery and death; hated the very smell of houses where it was. Had to get out in the fresh air before he choked. Now it was all waiting for him at home.

The waves of despair were worse than the waves that smashed in his face.

He grasped the oar firmly and wished to get lost forever; wished he was nowhere ...

*

It's always easy when you give-up. The waves no longer broke in his face. They came from behind in smooth surges, picking him up and driving him on. It seemed only minutes before he was into the mist, and then on the beach.

His legs were like lead; he couldn't lift his head even to be sick. When he finally managed to sit up, the first thing he noticed was that the oar was gone.

The mist was still down. And this wasn't any beach he knew. It was certainly not the beach by Monk's Heugh. This was smoother and bigger. It ran into the mist and out of sight in both directions.

"Hey!" he shouted. "Hey!"

The only answer was the calling of gulls somewhere to the south. If it was the south. If there *was* a south in nowhere; *Resurre* always gave you what you wanted.

He ran up the beach in a panic. After a hundred yards he came to sand-dunes with bent-grass on them. These, too, faded into the mist left and right.

He decided to turn south, towards the sun. All the time his eyes searched the ground, looking for clues to what time it was. Not that his diver's watch had stopped. It said quite clearly mid-day. But mid-day *when*? Cuddy's time? Viking time? He didn't want to meet the Vikings again. Especially stranded ashore in wet tee-shirt and underpants. But they'd be better than nothing.

But all he saw, as he veered between the dunes and the water's edge, was seaweed and driftwood. The driftwood had holes bored in it. But water had so worn the holes that he couldn't tell if they'd been bored by modern tools.

Then he saw the ringed plover, crouched under a clump of bent-grass, calling sharply for its mate as the wind ruffled its feathers. He laughed for joy. Ringed plovers meant RSPB bird-reserves. He knew where he was with ringed plovers.

Then the bird called again, sharp and lonely, and he realised he was nursing a false hope. Cuddy would have known ringed plovers, long before they appeared in any bird-recognition book. Ten thousand years was nothing to the ringed plover.

He moved towards it. It let him get within five yards before it flew off. Far too tame for a modern bird.

He plunged on through the dunes, looking, looking. But all he saw were the tracks of gulls; the broken eggshells of curlews. Each dune was exactly like the last. The sandy hollows between them were always empty, and the mist would not lift. At one o'clock, nearly mad with despair, he was still crossing dune after dune.

Nowhere in twentieth-century England could you walk for an hour and see no litter.

He had his nowhere, and he was terrified.

Then he saw the curved rusty rim, sticking a fraction out of the sand. His heart thudded; he was almost afraid to touch it. Suppose it was an abandoned war-axe, or a hand-forged ring?

He shut his eyes and grabbed.

He knew the feel, and the feel was all right, and he opened his eyes. In his hand was a crushed Coca-Cola tin.

Once he had one piece of litter, he found an abundance. Rotten apple-cores thick with sand; lollipopsticks, and finally a sunbrowned copy of the *Daily Mirror* dated August 1976. Then the mist lifted all in a rush. There were the Farnes, well south and end-on. There was Holy Island castle, surprisingly near.

He was on Ross Links nature-reserve, and all he had to fear was a long walk home in wet underpants.

He thought back to the brooding presence on Farne; the Cuddy his mind had refused to meet. He grinned wryly. Perhaps Cuddy hadn't wanted to meet him either. Why should he?

Michael Hendrey realised for the first time that he was not the centre of the universe.

But Cuddy had saved him from his own suicidal wish to be nowhere. Thanks, Cuddy, he thought. I didn't like nowhere.

Then the problems of being *somewhere* returned; the problems he had left behind two hours ago. The problems at home.

How was he going to cope? He broke out in a cold sweat. Being tough and clever wasn't enough. Kicking the world before it kicked you wasn't enough. That was all his mother had ever taught him, and look at the mess it had got her into.

You couldn't kick dead people, crying people, frightened people.

He supposed bitterly that Cuddy wouldn't bat an eyelid at drowned bodies and sobbing kids … but even Cuddy wasn't too keen on cranky women … Cuddy's way of life was no more help than Madeleine's. He'd better find his own way; by starting walking.

Just for a second he felt a ridiculous nostalgia for nowhere. It was clean and free and simple on Ross Links. But the wind blew coldly through his wet underpants and he knew he couldn't stay.

A path led inland through the dunes. He went up it like a condemned man walking to the scaffold.

There were two figures on the biggest dune; a small one in a blue dress and a tall one in yellow trousers. Both were looking out to sea. Behind them, crazily slewed in the sand, was a red sports-car.

He laughed and waved madly. Madeleine waved back. Sally put her arms up for a hug. Everyone was glad to see everyone.

Sally and Madeleine were pale and dishevelled, but they were warm, too. They'd all manage somehow; together.

"Thought you couldn't drive," said Mike, hiding his relief

in sarcasm.

"Twenty miles an hour, in third gear," said Madeleine, with a limp smile. "A bloke in a Mercedes followed us from Bamburgh, hooting all the way. He had plenty of chances to pass, but he preferred being a bastard. God," she wiped her forehead with a trembling hand, "there's a lot of hate loose on the roads. I wonder more people don't get killed."

"Weren't you scared that Cuddy …"

"You can only die once. If I'd stayed waiting one more hour in that house, I'd have gone bonkers. Where's Beth?"

"I got her ashore on Farne," said Mike. It sounded better than saying "I left her to be smashed to bits on the rocks".

But Madeleine understood.

"It's what she wanted, Mike. Just like Bertrand."

"You're very philosophical."

Madeleine shrugged. "I'm counting my blessings. I've got you back."

Mike buried his face in her binoculars. He looked across at Holy Island harbour, dreaming in the afternoon sun.

"It looks so peaceful – people are sunbathing. Is there really nothing we can do?"

"Nothing. I know how you feel. I keep wanting to ring up the police or the coastguard, or *somebody*!"

"There's a helicopter flying down the coast."

"It's only the R.A.F. Rescue job. It's out most days."

"So all we can do is wait?"

"Yes. This is as near the action as *we* can get."

"How can you stand it?"

"Women have been watching and waiting on this coast since before Cuddy's day. It's a knack. And," she added, poking Mike in the ribs, "I've had one bit of good luck turn up already. Or is it a piece of *bad* luck? There's coffee and sandwiches in the car, if you're hungry."

"Haven't got a spare pair of trousers, have you?"

XXI

Beth only allowed herself one look at Mike; to make sure he had the oar. She mustn't hang about; if she didn't move now, she'd never move at all.

She looked up. The rocks of the Stack were vertical as chimneys; grey clouds belched from the tops like smoke.

To do the whole climb was impossible; but there was one shelf she could reach, three feet higher. It was a start. Not easy though. The shelf she stood on sloped gently towards the sea and was glazed with green slime. As she raised her right foot, her left began slipping.

She tried clenching her left foot like a fist. It helped. But she'd have to make the step quickly, before the slipping really started.

She took one deep shuddering breath and stepped, both eyes shut. For one awful moment she had a foot on both rocks, and both slipping. Her hands started to ache beyond bearing. She could have sworn the rock bulged outwards, trying to push her into the sea.

Then, as her right foot found a ridge as small and painful as a razor blade, the slipping stopped. She brought up her left foot to join her right.

Her whole body was twitching like a terrified animal; she could not stop it. One step had taken all her strength.

Be still, said something inside. She clung to the rock with her eyes shut. The shaking went away. She opened her eyes and saw another rock two feet higher. The step-across was shorter, and the new rock seemed less slimy.

That was the way it went; every rock she gained revealed just one more. The higher she climbed, the drier the rocks became.

Until, fifty feet up, she noticed the smell: a sickly smell that came and went as the wind blew. Was it real? Or the cold affecting her nose?

Then she saw the fish. It was huge; wedged in a crevice facing her. It had eyes like sad melting marbles and its scales were dropping off. But the frightening thing was that three huge chunks had been bitten out of it, exposing the backbone. Above it were heaped a host of smaller fish, some bitten in half, some whole, some mere skeletons.

She gulped in sorrow and disgust. Then she noticed there was no other way upwards, except by sticking her feet into the crevice. She looked and looked; there was no other way. She put one foot in, and it slipped out again, in an avalanche of rotting fish. She had to reach in and pull out the remaining corpses one by one, and drop them down into the sea behind her. Even when she was finished, the crevice was thick with their slime. As she clawed her way up, it coated her arms and body.

But even the fish-crevice came to an end. She put her elbows on top and levered herself up onto a big ledge. She hung there, legs dangling in space.

Two birds sat watching her, one on the left and one on the right. They were as big as geese, with black fronts and bronze backs. Their feet were sharply webbed, and they sat on piles of black seaweed, holding open scarecrow wings. Worst were their beaks, long and down-curving.

Cormorants. She knew what had bitten through the great fish. She looked at her own goosepimpled arms.

But the birds only watched dully, necks drooping. When she grew bold enough to force her way between them, they backed off. Were they ill? Oil pollution? Then she remembered these seas were free of oil.

The going got easier, as the Stack sloped back to its top. But the rocks were thick with cormorant-droppings; it was like worming through stinking toothpaste. The birds were everywhere. She had to push them aside, but they merely watched with lack-lustre eyes. Were they *all* ill?

On top, she eased the ache in her back. Her bra was round her neck, a wet mass of rags. She tried to put it back on, but the strap had snapped. Still she left it hanging like a talisman; anything was better than nakedness. Without clothes you felt smaller and smaller. She hitched up her pants defensively, and took stock of the scene.

She was standing knee-deep in cormorants; they moved round her as quietly as farmhouse chickens. Constantly they watched the north. Her eyes followed theirs.

The main mass of Farne, like a hump-backed whale, filled the horizon. Just above its rim was a narrow band of golden sunlight. Everywhere else, black clouds smoked from the east.

Against the narrow band of gold was the outline of the round building Sally had showed her. That was where the cormorants were looking; something awful was going to happen there.

She looked down, and groaned aloud. She had forgotten the Stack was an isolated pinnacle; between it and the island proper there was only a low bridge of rock.

She would have to descend to sea-level and climb up all over again.

She began to push through the massed cormorants, terrified of treading on one.

But the worst part was making up her mind to descend. She found the birds parted in front of her, showing her a path; almost as if they were used to someone walking among them. And the rocks never went low enough to be slimy again. Soon she was on the long dry slabs leading to the top of the island.

Her pants split in two places, and then the elastic went. They kept falling round her ankles as she climbed. She took them off and kept them balled in her hand like a handkerchief.

The effect, she realised with a weak smile, was not seductive. Her body was criss-crossed with scratches and caked with slime. The cold had brought out livid splotches of purple and blue. Her feet were so numb that the rocks she walked on felt like foam-rubber.

Her body had become simply a machine for walking. Soon, it might be dead; food for cormorants. That should have been a wretched thought, but it was oddly soothing. No more endless trips to the dentist, or polio-jabs. No more girls giggling in the changing-room because her breasts were so small. It made things … simple.

She tried remembering her old life, but the memories blew away in the gale that whipped her drying hair. At first, she was afraid there'd be nothing left that was Beth. Then she realised these were memories she didn't want to keep. Schoolfriends making catty remarks about people and laughing; and she joining in the laugh in case the cattiness was turned on her … Her pride in her ten "O" levels; and with it the awful fear of failing, that would have returned with the "A" levels, and the degree, and the effort to get a university lectureship to please Bertrand. She didn't want any of it, nor the memory of kissing boys she didn't really like, for fear of being thought prudish.

She came to a shallow pool. Its golden surface was ringed with wind-ripples. She laughed, because it was the pool she'd sat beside with Mike, a thousand years away. It was still the same shape. Funny, the memories of Mike didn't blow away like the others. Mike shouting "Hallo, Sailor" or swearing at the Vikings, or telling lies to help her. Good things didn't blow away. She could remember her dogs at home. That much was safe.

She squatted in the pool to wash the slime off; the water was warmer than the wind.

She was tempted to go on washing when there was no

slime left. For the circular building was very near. In a few minutes she would be there.

She made herself walk on; across the old nests of eider-ducks. The wind was breaking them up, sending creamy eider-down streaming across the grass. But the ducks still crouched there, pressed to the ground, eyes looking towards the round hut.

She saw the hut was made of stones packed together with soil. Some of the stones would have taken ten men to lift. That book said Cuddy had lifted them alone. A stone cross showed above the wall; what Bertrand would have called the conventional Celtic pattern, all twisting lines.

There was a low door of boards, with a knothole through which darkness showed. She knocked timidly. No answer, above the wind. She thought: I'll knock three times then go away. Still no answer. But where else was there to go to? She went on walking round the circular wall, and came to a window with the same wooden shuttering. Paths led to the window. There was a worn place in the turf beneath. This was where people came and knocked.

She listened, and heard a restless rustling of straw, a babbling that might have been praying or someone raving in delirium.

She knocked again, very aware of her nakedness.

"*Ite Satanas!*" the voice boomed inside. Next second she was lying sprawled on the turf ten yards away; head whirling and body stinging all over. Yet she somehow knew the worst of the blow had missed her.

She got up shakily and shouted, "Hey, don't do that!"

"*Ite Satanas. Radix Malorum!*" This time she hit her hip on a boulder and felt sick. She decided to stay where she was and think.

Ite Satanas was Latin. It meant "begone Satan". *Radix Malorum* meant "the root of evil", which was what the old monks called women. She was being mistaken for a devil disguised as a woman; like the ones that haunted St Anthony as he lay dying in the Egyptian desert.

She surveyed her body ruefully. St Anthony's devils must have looked a lot more dishy! Then she got angry. She was not a devil, and the creature inside ought to *know* that. Well, she would tell it; she spoke Latin too.

She marched up to the window, trying to forget her nakedness. She made the Sign of the Cross and shouted:

"Amica Christi sum!"

Next second, she wished she hadn't. The whole island seemed to tilt under a hammer-blow. The clouds blew to the left, then to the right, then straight at her. Her head seemed split down the middle, and her two eyes saw things from two different viewpoints.

Eider-ducks rose in droves and were flung about the sky like autumn leaves. No wonder they all looked so ill, if this kept happening to them.

Then she was clinging to the turf with clawed fingers, as the island seemed to turn upside-down, and clouds boiled beneath her.

Gradually, the hammer-blows grew less and ceased. The terrified birds returned to their nests in silence. Too much silence. She returned to the window.

The praying had stopped. There was only heavy painful breathing. A farmyard smell came through the cracks in the shutters, and worse: the smell Rover had had, after the cat scratched him and the wound turned septic, and the vet came too late.

She suddenly wanted to help. She pushed at the shutter, but it was too strong. So was the door. But a leather bucket lay in the doorway, with a wooden ladle. It was bone-dry. How long had the man inside been without water? Filling his bucket was the least she could do. She set off back to the pool.

She was returning when she saw something move on the

skyline. Too big for a bird. It had four legs and something on its back that she couldn't make out against the sunset. Now there were four … black goats. The devils had come across the sands from Wideopen.

She wanted to stand stock-still till they went away. But she somehow realised that was what they wanted, too. So she went on walking, holding the bucket with both hands. They closed in round her.

The worst thing was, she couldn't believe they were real. They were so absurdly small: black baby feet in their stirrups; black baby hands clenched round spears; no faces inside their cowls, just shadow with the glint of eyes. They were like something people saw on a bad LSD trip. She wondered if cold and hunger were giving her hallucinations.

She couldn't make the Sign of the Cross, because her hands were full. She tried shouting "*Ite Satanas*". It had no effect. There were dozens round her now; and dozens more hounding and tormenting the eider-ducks who ran in circles, their poor heads near the ground.

"Look! Look!" shrieked the devils, pointing in the air with their spears. She knew she shouldn't look; but she had to.

A huge boulder was falling straight on her. She ducked. The boulder never landed. But she had lost half the water in her bucket. That was what the devils wanted; they shrieked with glee.

After that, she went on walking towards the circular building no matter what. Chasms gaped at her feet. She strode into them, seemed to fall endlessly, and then found herself still walking on the unbroken grass. Stabbing pains shot through her neck and back. Was it just the weight of the bucket, or the devils' spears? She did not turn to find out.

Ahead, the circular building was surrounded by a horde of devils. Flames roared up from walls and shutters. The higher the flames shot, the more the devils yelled. But she pushed through. The goats' harsh hides scraped her legs. Their sharp little hoofs bit at her feet. Goat-stench filled her nostrils. But she kept on, and threw the water at the shutter with all her force.

Inside, the sick man groaned. The flames went out, leaving no trace of burning. The devils began to back away.

Straw rustled, as if someone was standing up. Behind, she could hear goat-hoofs everywhere, fading into silence. When she looked, there wasn't one in sight.

Behind the shutter, a weary voice spoke.

"*Femina bona es!*" "You are a virtuous woman." The Latin was easy. "Go. I must keep vigil and pray."

"You are ill. Can I help?"

"Nothing. Go!"

There was no disobeying that voice. She went. The only path led to the Haven and back into the sea.

Just before the Haven, though, was a thatched building on the right. That must be the hospitium where visitors stayed. On impulse, she opened the door.

It was dark inside, but smelled sweetly of the sea. The floor was dry sand. There were beds of dry seaweed in the corners. On the table was a jug of water and a loaf of bread. The loaf had a cross on it, like the one in Uncle Henry's attache case.

She tore off some bread and ate it. No new thunderbolt of rage smote her. She drank from the jug; the water was flat and stale, but the island's peace continued.

Then she saw the monk's robe hanging on the back of the door, grey and patched. Suddenly it seemed important to cover her cold nakedness. The robe was scratchy and far too big, but warm.

She collapsed on the seaweed, dead with weariness. Her last thought was how could she sleep while her father sailed to his death? Then she remembered that her father was in another time.

XXII

She wakened to the sound of distant Latin; it sounded like a psalm. Then she realised she'd been hearing psalms all night through her dreams, like the motor-traffic on the main road at home. Sometimes the chanting grew loud, as dragging footsteps passed her door. It made her feel safe.

She opened the door, onto a blue morning with big waves breaking. The tide was up, making Wideopen seem small and far away. One solitary devil was in view, picking its way through the pools as nervously as an outfaced cat. Even a dying saint was too much for them, awake. And it seemed that this saint never slept. No wonder he was dying.

She cast longing eyes at the circular building. But as she looked the psalm grew louder, in a way that firmly meant "No".

She ate dry bread, drank stale water, and wondered what to do. She felt well, but stiff; perhaps a walk would help.

Walking wasn't easy. She rolled up the sleeves of the robe, but they kept falling down over her hands; and if she couldn't hold up the skirt, she couldn't walk at all. Besides, the moment she stepped outside, the eiders left their nests and flocked to her. Then, at close range they retreated, baffled. It was the robe they were flocking to, not her.

Even so, they insisted on accompanying her, in a growing flock. Other birds came: shy dunlin from the beach and shyer redshanks from the pools. Gulls hovered on the wind. There were even rabbits. It was embarrassing. Beth wished she knew what they wanted.

What season of the year was it? There were no young birds, or wildflowers. The grass had the weary look it wears from

November to March. The wind was cold enough for either; she was glad of the robe.

She reached the northwest tip of the island, Churn Gut, and had to sit down. Big waves were rolling in from the north-east, rushing up the Gut, and spouting ninety feet in the air. It was exciting at first. Then it got monotonous, like the ticking of some great clock. There was no warmth in the rocks, no kindness in the waves. She could die here, and moulder to a skeleton, and blow away to dust, and the waves would go on running remorselessly up the Gut. For a thousand years, till Michael came.

Despair swept over her. She'd done what she'd set out to do, and it changed nothing. Cuddy would no more listen than her father. They were like two heartless masculine millstones grinding together, with her trapped between. All she had accomplished was to trap herself, in time *and* space.

She looked across to the mainland. Instead of the usual fields, oakwoods marched to the brink of the sea. Even if she could swim back without the help of the oar, it would be a different land. Full of churls and thegns and little blood-thirsty kings who fought without ceasing. Even if she wasn't raped, or burned as a witch, she'd have to break her back with work sixteen hours a day just to get enough to eat. And probably die of bearing fourteen children. She wanted nothing this time could offer. She wished she was dead.

Then a different thought came into her head.

How can a man on an island take himself seriously? For if he is wild one day, like these waves, he knows God will make him calm the next. There is no way he can alter either the waves or his moods …

For as the waves beat against the rock forever, and the rock is not changed … so, however much he batter himself against the Almighty Father, He shall remain, his rock and fortress forever …

She started up wildly, and looked around. That wasn't one

of *her* thoughts. That wasn't the kind of thought she had. Was she going potty? It was lonely enough to drive you potty.

Be still. That thought was sent to me, in the cave beneath your feet, where I hid three days during a storm … I was afraid the storm would never end, and the ship from Lindisfarne never come, and I should starve.

Then I saw a gull riding the stormy sea quite unharmed, though great waves broke all round … and I knew that my wretched faith was weaker than the gull's, which is a brute bird …

Then, I was young. Now I would rejoice if the ship did not come, for the strengthening of my faith.

Was she having delusions? What Bertrand would call schizophrenic hallucinations? There was only one way to find out. She climbed down the cliff, looking for the cave.

It was there; small and wretched with green slime, but where the strange thought had said. She returned to her rock and sat down primly, hands in her lap. The sound of psalms had ceased in the round building. The saint, in his own way, was condescending to talk.

Why did you not believe me about the cave?

She blushed. "My father trained me to check facts."

Your father?

Was it coincidence that a cloud came over the sun, and the waves' roar increased?

"Please help my father."

How can I help your father? He is living his life in the way that seems best to him, as I am living the life that seems best to me.

"He's trying to save the Vikings."

The sky grew darker still.

THAT IS A LIE. He is trying to save his own pride. His pride is a tool in the hands of the Ancient Enemy, to torment my last days. His death is one more for my wretched soul to repent. I have too many already. There were many Vikings.

"But you don't have to kill any of them. You can change things. You healed my sister's hand."

"*I am not a sorcerer.*" The wind tore savagely at her robe, full of cold knives. "*Your sister is among the living. I can change the living. The Vikings have been scattered bones for ten years. I have repented them ten years. I cannot change the dead, for their sake or mine. That is sorcery!*"

The thoughts coming into her head grew wild and confused. It was like having your ear too close to a defective amplifier; agony.

"Is my father already dead?"

I do not ... do not ... not ... do not know. Do not ... do not ... torment me, daughter, in the hour of my death.

"Please use your power!"

Power ... power ... power ... always they want my power. Why do you think I hid in this tiny dwelling on a rock, where the waves of swelling ocean surround me ... and shut me from the sight of men? But even here ... I am not free ... from the snares of the deceiving world ... even here I fear ... lest the love of power tempt me ... from the strife of the hermit's life I love.

Shall I ever know peace? I asked the brethren to bury me here, near my oratory ... on the eastern side of the Holy Cross I have erected ... in the stone coffin which the venerable abbot Cudda gave me.

But they will not. For the power in my bones they will take me to Lindisfarne ... bury me in a tomb by the altar of their church. By my bones, many will be healed ... great wealth will come to the brethren ... lawless men, thieves and murderers will flee to my bones for sanctuary, and will drag down the brethren to worldly thoughts. All this I told them, but they would not heed ... no peace ... no peace ...

The wind fell, with the sound of weeping.

"Can I help?"

You have, daughter. In my miserable pride, I sought to fight the fight of Christ by my own powers, to the end. And in my miserable pride the devils nigh overcame me as I slept. From this you saved me. I am grateful.

"What will you do now?"

I will leave this place of strife and wait in the hospitium till the brethren come. There is too much sweat of devils here.

"How will the brethren know?"

They are coming already, across the sea. Farewell, daughter.

"Please save my father. I need him so much."

You have your Father in Heaven.

"No, no. My real father."

"Why do you need him? He is a small man. Already you are greater, in charity and long-suffering and prayer."

"But ... but ... he has looked after me ever since I was a little girl."

No! You have looked after him since you were a little girl. Now he holds you back from the Way. You will do your great work when he is gone from the earth.

"Oh, please ... I shall be so lonely ..."

Pray to the Father. In Him only there is no loneliness.

And with the words came a wave of sorrow that swamped Beth's as the incoming tide swamps a rock-pool. The sorrow of the saint.

Now, I would go to the Father, but the brethren will take my body ... They will bind me to the earth ... no rest, no rest ...

Silence, which Beth could not will herself to break. Then a psalm rose stumbling from the round building. She could hear the desolation in it, and something very close to despair. But it went on.

As she would go on, when her father was dead. When he was no more than a fading photograph, old letters and a library of out-of-date books. When he grew smaller in her memory every year.

She had lived for her father. Now she must simply live. She walked dully to the Haven; leaving the island any other way meant jumping over a cliff.

As she walked she saw the devils coming up the shore. But they were ghostly and flickering now, like old cinema newsreel; and they paid her no attention as they passed, heading for the round building. Were they real, or inside Cuddy's head? Was *she* inside Cuddy's head? She couldn't work it out. Her own head ached to bursting.

As she passed the hospitium she turned aside, made the bed tidy and hung the robe back on the door. Then she walked down the sand, shivering with more than cold.

Resurre's oar lay on the sand, one end swinging in the surf. She took it and swam out into the Kettle. She was not alone. She could feel seals moving past her in the water, and the air was alive with terns. Soon, water and air were so full of living things she became almost afraid. Where were they all going?

There was a boat coming towards her, riding the waves like a storm-tossed gull. It had one small sail. But it wasn't Bertrand, because sail and hull were new and white; with gilded lettering round the prow.

She pushed in closer, trying to read the lettering. It was difficult, for the press of sea-beasts and her head ringing with the calling of birds; but she managed it.

Then the boat swept past, full of monks with tears falling down their faces. The hymn they were singing was *Ave Maris Stella*. Then the sea-beasts turned to follow in a smooth flurry of wet fur, and she was left alone.

The lettering round the prow had read:

RESURRECTIO VITAQUE SUM
I am the Resurrection and the Life

It was *Resurre*, brand-new.

It was the boat that was going to bring Cuddy home.

Then the mist came down, and the waves of time bore her on. She felt like a mouse inside the workings of Big Ben.

XXIII

Beyond the mist, Bertrand plunged into darkness. He wondered if the saint was playing tricks on him. Whatever Vikings did, they didn't navigate rocky unknown coasts in the middle of the night.

Bertrand smirked. If the saint was cheating, that reduced him straight away – to no better than the little boy who upset the table when he was losing at chess. Over the centuries, the Church had always cheated; changing the rules of the game whenever things got too difficult.

Then his eyes grew accustomed to the dark, and he saw the eastern sky was slightly lighter, with the false dawn. *That* was more like it. The Vikings would have located the monastery the previous day, and lain out to sea again; to make a dawn attack and catch the monks asleep.

He was prepared to wait; and wouldn't waste the waiting time. He would put *Resurre* through her paces. It had been easy to deduce that the boat sailed primarily on willpower. The children had needed the steering-oar because their wills were weaker, not yet disciplined, but he could do without it. It was only a matter of learning a new technique, and he'd always been quick at that.

The simplicity of oarless steering pleased and surprised him. Foam creamed from the sharp bow; he must be doing fifteen knots. And she could turn on a sixpence, and sail so close to the wind it was a dream. It was more like flying an aeroplane. He was sure he could get twenty knots, even thirty knots, out of her.

There was a roar of breakers. He was hard against the sandbanks of Old Law, at the mouth of Holy Island harbour. He just managed to turn out to sea in time. Ahah, you don't catch me that way, Cuddy! It would be so convenient to have me capsized and helpless, as the attack went in, half a mile away across the harbour.

Might as well get to know the harbour; shoals and landing-places. He learned them thoroughly in the dim light. There was no sign of life from the monastery, behind its round stone wall. Monks were dozy sheep; so unworldly they didn't even set a night-watchman. Really, they deserved all they got. You needed all your wits about you in this wicked world. But perhaps their eyes were firmly fixed on the next. And when they got themselves slaughtered by their own stupidity, the Church would call them martyrs. There were no martyrs, only failures.

Well, that was one more job done. He was ready for anything now. But he wouldn't venture too far out to sea. It would be too easy for old Cuddy to raise a squall from the north, and drive him beyond Farne till it was all over. Play it tight, boy; keep your cards close to your chest.

The birds were waking. He could hardly believe there were so many. Huge flocks of terns flew shrieking, in their dipping hysterical search for fish. Funny about terns: you always sensed they were around, before you heard them. They sent a kind of electric excitement ahead.

Now there were bigger birds among them, diving on them, pursuing them remorselessly till they dropped their catch of fish: arctic skuas, cunning thieving predators. They would give the terns something to be hysterical about!

Now the sea was afloat with eider families. Big convoys of twenty or thirty chicks, held in tight formation by ducks and drakes, front and rear. He admired the eiders' discipline; they looked like shipping convoys in the War. Ahah! Convoy formation needed! A couple of skuas were having a go at the chicks.

He stopped the boat to watch. The eider-chicks closed up even tighter, until they were a continuous brown mat rising and falling across the waves.

In came the skuas, diving straight for the mat, a foot above the waves, trying to scatter the convoy. At the last moment, the eider-drake at the back beat his wings and rose vertically in the water. The skuas swerved away, and circled for another attack. Against the eider's great wings they looked suddenly frail, but here they came again.

He watched enthralled. The skuas avoided the great beating wings first by feet and then by inches. The eider-chicks began to scatter as the pressure built up. The ducks pressed them together again, calling frantically. Any minute now …

Then a skua cut it too fine. The eider-drake's black wing just tipped him as he passed; but it was enough. The skua cartwheeled across the wave-tops at fifty miles an hour and dissolved into a limp bobbing mass. The mat of eiders passed over and round him. The other skua flew slowly away.

Bertrand urged the boat gently across to the floating body. Hard luck, you vicious bastard, he thought, full of wild satisfaction.

Then Bertrand remembered where he was, and looked seawards, and swore. The sun was fully up. Right against it, hard to see through watering eyes, were the black sails of three Viking-ships. Cuddy had nearly got the better of him; using Cuddy's ducks, of course.

But not quite; there was still time. He sent *Resurre* skimming across the harbour.

She grounded with a jarring thud, on a little beach he'd picked out below the monastery. He didn't wait to moor her; just ran for the monastery gate. It opened with one kick; it wasn't even barred.

Nothing stirred in the muddy courtyard, or between the thatched huts. It might have been some wretched African village, except for the cross on top of the biggest hut, and a bell in a rickety wooden belfry. He pulled the bell so hard that the belfry threatened to collapse on top of him.

Little men came staggering out of the huts, gape-eyed and yawning. Each had a bald front to his head. They wore brown robes, with bits of straw sticking to them. They all looked exactly alike. He couldn't get over how *small* they were.

They stared at him, jabbering in an unknown language. One or two began making the Sign of the Cross vigorously, as if to ward him off.

But he pointed through the open gate. One of the Viking-ships sailed into view round the harbour-point, and that was message enough.

There was chaos. Some flung themselves flat on their faces and began to babble Latin. Others dived back into the huts and emerged carrying gold-bound books and silver cups; then ran to and fro aimlessly. One dropped his book and it burst apart; vellum leaves, marvellously interwoven with red and blue, drifted round the courtyard in the morning wind. Some monks clutched each other, weeping. A sensible few ran as fast as they could out of the gate.

Bertrand found himself despising them utterly. They were like chickens with their heads cut off. So much for monastic discipline! They could have taken a lesson from the eider-ducks!

He could see how they got massacred. They were simply asking for it. He felt like chasing them himself, shouting boo at them, kicking them up the backside. Any *real* man would despise such creatures, feel like tormenting them. How could the Vikings be blamed?

The Vikings! They must be stopped; for their *own* sakes.

He ran down the shore trying to calm himself. He was not as calm as he would have liked. The battle between eiders and skuas had excited him; the panic of the monks made him worse. He took deep breaths; he must be totally rational, logical.

But it was hard. He realised he was running with his hands stiff as boards, the ridge of muscle on their outsides hardened ready for a blow. I have come to make peace, he thought, not fight on a Judo-mat; be calm, be calm.

Halfway down the beach he halted. All three Viking ships were pulled up on the sand. Vikings were streaming ashore briskly. He held up his hands and shouted, "Stop!"

That was stupid. How would they know what "Stop" meant? But the ones heading straight for him hesitated. At least the upraised hands must be a universal signal. Interesting … was there need for research into the universality of human gesture?

But the Vikings on either side did not stop. They gave him a wide berth and ran on towards the monastery. With an awful single-mindedness. Like the skuas.

"Stop!" he shouted again. "Stop, you idiots. Go in there and you're dead men."

They paid not the slightest heed, and vanished through the gate. There was an awful scream; the first column of flame shot skywards.

He realised he was surrounded by a crowd of men, standing some feet back and eyeing him curiously. He surveyed them in turn. He was not particularly impressed. Somehow he had expected huge figures with wings on their helmets, and great flowing beards. He realised now that such figures existed only in the Victorian history-books he'd read as a child. How foolish!

These men were bigger than the monks, but not much. He was a head taller than the biggest. And they didn't look so much fearsome as *nasty*. Like a mob of Irish tinkers dressed up badly for a fancy-dress ball. Only one had a helmet with rather stubby horns; most had no helmets at all. Their swords had dents in their cutting edges, and were rusty.

They smelt abominably. And they were a kind of walking catalogue of forgotten diseases. One had a neck swollen to a barrel with goitre. Others had the sunken chests and bandy legs of rickets. Their teeth were falling out with scurvy, and one man's eyes showed the milky blindness of a cataract. Bertrand felt unclean just looking at them.

They had two prisoners. One was a wretch of a fisher-lad from some outlying hut, but the other was a lady, with long braided hair and fine garments. She was tied to the leader's wrist by a leather thong, and did not look as if she had been enjoying life for some time.

Bertrand disliked the leader on sight. He had a squint, so it was impossible to tell whether he was looking at you or not. A sword-cut across his bull-shoulder had healed without the benefit of surgery. He looked both stupid and cunning; Bertrand had often met his sort. Bertrand stared at him until his squint-eyes dropped. This was not lost on the other Vikings, who muttered.

At that point, Bertrand made a mistake. Perhaps it was the increasing noise of flames and screaming that was coming from behind. Bertrand's presence here was making no difference at all. So he grabbed the leader by the shoulders, turning him to look towards Farne.

"Get your men to *stop*. There's someone on that island –"

The leader flung Bertrand's hands away with surprising strength. He and Bertrand glared at each other. Then the leader drew back and shouted something.

Two Vikings pulled the fisher-lad forward. They forced him to his knees, forced his head and neck to the ground, twisting his arms cruelly behind his back.

Bertrand showed he was not impressed by such pointless bullying. Next moment the leader raised his sword and hacked the lad's head from his shoulders. Blood from the severed neck spouted over Bertrand's sandalled feet. It was shockingly hot. The poor head lay on its side, mouth twitching slightly as if it was still alive. The leader savoured the look of shock on Bertrand's face. He made the mistake of thinking it was fear. He shouted to his men again.

Hands clutched Bertrand's elbows. He leapt forward to

avoid them, and, without thinking, landed in a crouch on the balls of his feet, hands in the fighting position by his sides.

That was also a universal gesture. The leader understood. With a slow smile of enjoyment he slipped the thong that held the lady-captive from his wrist, and went into an odd lop-sided sort of hunch that was obviously *his* favourite fighting position.

After hundreds of Judo-lessons, Bertrand had been well-trained to cope with attackers with a knife or club; this was halfway between. Besides, the man's style was pathetic. He stood flat-footed, with his legs too widely splayed for quick movement. He could easily be caught off balance. More than that, he had closed his right eye, the one with the squint. That would spoil his judgement of distance; it also made him blind on the right side. Best of all, the Viking was too confident. He thought he'd won already.

On the other hand, he had the advantage of his armour. His helmet had a nasal, protecting the vulnerable nose. He had a collar of iron rings that protected the vulnerable spots on his neck. He would be hard to kill with bare hands. Kill? *Kill?*

Bertrand was so disgusted with himself that the Viking's first stroke almost got him. He turned sideways just in time. The sword tore his smock down the back from top to bottom.

But after that, the fight was just a pattern, like a rally at tennis. No time to feel emotion. The Viking hewed forward again, the same clumsy stroke. While he was off balance, Bertrand knocked his helmet spinning with one back-handed flick. The surrounding Norsemen grunted with excitement.

Bertrand pretended to half-trip, and staggered back. The maddened Viking made the same stroke a third time. Perhaps he only had one stroke?

Bertrand used the same back-handed flick to the nose. He

felt the nasal bones break under his hand like Hong-Kong plastic. The Viking stood up straight, as the fragments of nasal bone entered his brain. He said something in gargling surprise. Then blood streamed from his mouth and he fell. His chest heaved once, and he was dead.

The ring of Vikings roared; not with rage but excitement. Two dragged the body away by the feet. Immediately another man leapt in to face Bertrand. He was younger, with pale hair. He was much swifter on his feet, and preferred a dagger.

Round and round they went, feet dragging through the sand. The other Vikings began calling to each other. Bertrand wondered if they were making bets on who would win.

He was not sure himself. The new man had watched him fight, seen how he killed the other. He was learning all the time. There was real intelligence in his eyes, and that made Bertrand reluctant to kill. Intelligence was so rare in this world … even misplaced intelligence.

Then the misplaced intelligence landed a slash that set Bertrand's shoulder dripping blood. The fighting animal in Bertrand took over again, and landed a kick that put the Viking on the sand. Bertrand seized his dagger-arm and broke it, before he could recover. Then he turned away feeling sick with disgust.

It was nearly the last thing he ever did. Only a shout from the crowd warned him in time. The fallen Viking had picked up his dagger with the other hand, and was coming at him again, damaged arm drooping like a broken wing.

It wasn't difficult to club him senseless; but then a third man stepped into the circle.

Now Bertrand knew despair. They would keep on till he collapsed exhausted. He couldn't kill them all. Already his legs were shaking and his eyes near-blind with sweat. And the circle round him had thickened with men holding looted gold. The destruction of the monastery was over. The Vikings had had their sport with the monks. Now they thought

Bertrand much more fun. He could hear the pack-yell in their throats he'd always hated; the sound fox-hounds make. There was no reasoning with a pack; a hundred bodies and only one bloody sub-human mind. Deep inside, Bertrand thought:

You were right to drown them, Cuddy; you were right all along.

As if in answer, a gust of rain splattered in his face. He glanced towards the east.

A black cloud lay over the sea, trailing a curtain of rain. The cloud grew perceptibly as he watched, and lightning flickered. The gusts grew stronger. There was a grinding and clattering from the beach. One Viking-ship had broached sideways and was hammering against its neighbour. All three masts were rocking wildly. The waves breaking on the beach were already two feet high.

Fear showed in every Viking face. Without ships they became mere fugitives, to be hunted down at leisure by the local eorl and his warband; to be skinned alive and have their hides nailed to the church door.

They turned and ran to their destruction.

Bertrand leaned against a post and watched. The only difference his intervention had made was one body lying on the sand, and blood seeping through his own jerkin. He watched the Vikings struggling to get their ships launched. They looked as feeble as the monks had done. He felt no pity. They deserved all they got.

Then a gust of wind came so strong he had to cling to the post to stay upright. He looked to sea again, and saw a wave as high as a house: a wave that would reach where he stood, that would sweep the coast of Holy Island bare to the tree-roots.

He didn't care. He too would get what he deserved, for being wrong, wrong, wrong. Wrong about everything. Cuddy's storm existed, therefore Cuddy's God existed.

Atheist rational man was as obsolete as the dinosaur. Let him pass with the dinosaurs; Bertrand didn't want to go on living in a world in which God existed; it was far too complicated to start all over again.

Then he saw a flash of blonde hair down by the longships. It was the woman prisoner. Two men were trying to drag her aboard by the thong on her wrist. She was resisting vigorously, digging her feet in the sand.

She was innocent; she didn't deserve to die. There *was* one last useful thing for atheist man to do.

Bertrand ran into the surf. Two blows and the thong was in his hand. The woman recognised him and stopped struggling; she probably thought him some Anglo-Saxon hero, some unsung Beowulf.

He grasped her wrist and ran towards where he had left *Resurre*. Waves flung themselves against the back of his legs, trying to push him under. Half the time the woman was crawling, or afloat, but he kept dragging her by the wrist.

Resurre was still there, just flung further up the beach; tossing impatiently like a restive horse. He had a shrewd idea that *Resurre* could look after herself; she was immortal.

As they clambered aboard, he glanced out to sea. One Viking ship was lying on her side in the shallows. As he watched, the mast snapped, and she turned over onto the heads of her crew. But the other two were well out to sea, oars flailing. Lightning flashed incessantly, making the whole scene flicker black-and-white like an early movie.

Then, beyond the longships, he saw the great wave. It was much higher than a house. It swallowed Steel End as if it had been a sandcastle, and swept across the Heugh, its hunger unappeased. Bertrand turned *Resurre* to face it.

It was like climbing a hill of breaking foam. Then, with *Resurre* balanced on top, the wave swept across the charred remains of the monastery, buried the rocky fang of Hobthrush, and rolled on towards the mainland shore.

Wave followed wave followed wave. Each left *Resurre* wallowing in a trough to await its successor. Bertrand didn't doubt that *Resurre* was immortal. The sail did not split, no rope gave way. But that was no reassurance. One wave could capsize her and tip her passengers into the sea; the next could right her again, leaving her unharmed and her crew drowned.

But if he kept her bow to the waves ... He bent every effort of his will, and thought he could sense the saint's opposing will, in the power of the storm.

So he kept his mind on the Anglo-Saxon lady; kept the single thought: *Innocent, Innocent*, echoing in his mind as each wave came upon them.

Just as Bertrand felt his last ounce of will drain away; just as the greatest wave of all reared up; just as the lee shore of the mainland loomed ...

They were floating on three-inch ripples. The sun was shining hot. He could see car-windscreens winking on the Holy Island causeway. There were people on the beach, sunbathing in orange loungers. A transistor-radio was giving a commentary on the last test match.

Bertrand turned the boat gently away from the beach, looked towards Farne, and thought: Beat you, you Christian bastard!

If Cuddy heard, he did not reply. The sky stayed blue from horizon to horizon.

Bertrand smiled at the woman. She could do with a wash, but she really was a splendid creature, tall and full-bosomed.

The woman returned a brief grateful smile. But she stared around nervously; at the bright cars on the causeway and the transistors on the beach.

"*Dracones?*" she asked, swallowing. Dragons? Bertrand took her hand in a reassuring grip, and tried to think of the Latin for "chariots". But the woman pulled her hand away, and went on staring at the motor-cars. Best get her out to sea; where she would calm down and he could break it to her gently.

Then came a more raucous sound. *Blat-blat-blat-blat*. Sharp blows on the ears, so you could almost feel the pressure in the air.

The dragon came slowly towards them, twenty feet above the waves. It was bright yellow, and its wings glinted transparent in the sun, like a dragonfly's. It had glinted bulbous eyes like a dragonfly too. Only it was fifty feet long.

The woman screamed in utter terror.

"It's only a helicopter," said Bertrand.

Too late. The woman grabbed the boat's sail, trying to steer away from the dragon …

And the wave was towering over them bigger than a house, and the gale was tearing at their hair, and Bertrand repeated *Innocent* just once. He had no will left to fight.

XXIV

"What's that?" said Mike.

"What's what?" asked Madeleine, heaving herself off the sand-dune with a jerk, and groping for the binoculars.

"Small dark boat with a single sail. Appeared out of nowhere. It's *Resurre* – it must be."

Madeleine focussed the glasses and yelped, "It is *Resurre!* And Bertrand. And, do you know what? He's got a girl with him!"

"Is it Beth?"

Mike could feel his heart pounding. Maybe everything was going to be all right.

"No, it's a blonde. Isn't that just typical! He goes off to change the course of history, frightens me half to death, and what do I find him doing? Joy-riding with some dolly-bird he's picked up on the beach. Wait till he comes home. Come in, number twenty-two, your time is up!"

Mike shook his head in bafflement. Her words were angry – old Madeleine words – but her face was young with joy so that he could hardly bear to look at it. Then his mother was looking through the binoculars again.

"That ... female's got her hair in pigtails. She's wearing one of those awful embroidered smocks out of the *Observer*. Bertrand always has had a weakness for that type ... oh!"

She began to swing the glasses and fiddle with the focus. "I've lost them."

"Don't bother," said Mike. But it was ten minutes before Madeleine would admit defeat. Then her shoulders drooped.

"Anyway, we know he's still alive."

Well, we did ten minutes ago, thought Mike. Or a thousand years ago. Or something.

"There's a police-car driving down the beach," said Madeleine. "This is obviously a day for wonders."

It did look odd, spurting down the flat wet sand with an oar sticking out of its back window. Then an arm waved out of the front. The car stopped. A policeman got out in his shirt-sleeves, followed by a girl who appeared to be wearing a dark-blue mini-dress with sergeant's stripes on the sleeve.

"It's *Beth*!" said Mike.

They hurried over.

"What seems to be the trouble, officer?" said Madeleine briskly.

The sergeant blushed to the roots of his hair.

"I ... er ... found this young woman wandering on the beach in ... a distressed condition, madam." It was obvious that Beth was stark naked under his tunic.

"She had this oar with her," added the sergeant.

"Whore?" said Madeleine crossly. "*Which* whore?"

"*Oar*, madam," said the sergeant, blushing again and gesturing at the rear window. "The young woman says she's your daughter."

"Well, yes," said Madeleine.

"I'll have to charge her, madam. On account of her wandering in her ... distressed condition. We know you people come up here on holiday to enjoy yourselves. We like to leave people to enjoy themselves in their own way. My inspector is a most liberal-minded man ... but there are *limits*, madam!"

Madeleine glanced at Beth, who was nearly in tears, and took the sergeant aside. Mike heard her say, "Rather disturbed ... we thought her little sister was drowned ... now her father's missing in a boat ..."

Light dawned on the sergeant.

"You the family from Monk's Heugh, madam?"

"Yes."

The sergeant backed away. He thinks we're *all* nuts, thought Mike. And I don't blame him.

"Well, perhaps I can waive the charge this time, madam ... it's obviously a special case. But ..."

"But what?" asked Madeleine.

"I have to ... have my uniform back, madam. I'm on duty ..."

Madeleine whipped off her own long-line cardigan and gave it to Beth; leaving herself clad only in slacks and a fetching lace brassiere.

The sergeant retreated halfway back to his Panda, clutching his uniform jacket firmly. He had noticed that Mike was wearing only a shirt and underpants ...

"I should ... watch the weather, madam. It can turn cold very quickly, even on the warmest day. It's the north-east winds, madam. Don't want all your family catching cold now, do we?"

Then he was gone up the beach, as fast as a revved third gear would take him.

"How did you know where to find us?" said Madeleine to Beth.

"I don't ... don't know," wailed Beth, and burst into tears.

Madeleine said, "Look at your legs, girl! You're scratched to pieces."

"It doesn't hurt much, really."

"Why are you crying then?"

"Because you're all here, and you're all so nice and *small!*"

"Bloody teenagers!" said Madeleine. "And especially bloody *female* teenagers." But she was just swearing to hide her happiness again. Then she got all sergeant-major.

"Right. Home and bed for you, Beth. I'll come back for you and Sally, Mike. And if I find either of you has moved an inch, I'll *crucify* you."

She extricated the car from the sand-dune, making it sound

like the whole Battle of Britain, and drove off at something approaching her old pace. Some of Cuddy's effects seemed to be wearing off.

Mike took Sally down to the water's edge to skim stones across the waves. It *seemed* a pretty safe thing to do.

XXV

Bertrand closed his eyes and waited stoically for death. But the boat rose and fell three times, and death didn't come. If he didn't open his eyes soon, he was in more danger of being seasick.

He opened his eyes and looked for the next wave. It was big, but not higher than a house. The next seemed smaller. To the east, the black cloud was breaking up. It had only been a tremendous thunder-squall.

He looked at the woman. She held the sail competently, quite unafraid. She was even smiling slightly; perhaps dismissing the helicopter as a momentary hallucination. Just one of those things.

The waves got steadily smaller. They were now sailing under a blue sky; but only the sky was normal. Sea and land seemed to have changed places. For the sea was afloat with land-things; uprooted bushes and dead sheep. Whereas the shore where they landed was buried in seaweed, already steaming and stinking in the sun. It had an awesome deep smell, as if the sea had vomited.

Pressed down among the weed lay the bodies of skuas and Vikings, intermingled. Flat, wet and dead. Bertrand noticed the body of the man whose arm he'd broken; then the body of the man he'd killed. Both looked drowned now, like the rest. Time was healing its wounds; as it was healing the bloody slash in Bertrand's shoulder. The waves had washed that clean, and the salt was drawing the skin together.

He followed the woman up to where the monastery had stood. Three little brown men were hunting the wreckage for what they could salvage. They looked like bedraggled redshanks, wading the pools.

They talked to the woman, in a language he couldn't understand. Then they smiled at him shyly, bowed deeply, and patted him on the back. They seemed grateful.

But you can only say so much with smiles, and they soon went back to their salvage operations. Bertrand found a drying rock, and sat down in the sun.

More little brown monks appeared. The Viking massacre hadn't been as bad as he thought. Most of the monks must have fled inland, where the dunes had absorbed the worst of the waves.

Then boats put out from the mainland, full of people anxious to help. The first thing they did was to tie together two large pieces of wood, to make a cross. This they set up where the monastery had been. Bertrand noted ironically that the pieces of wood were shattered spars from the Viking-ships.

The lady brought a man over to see him. He had fierce blue eyes, gold bracelets and good fighting muscles. He managed to look both grateful and jealous at the same time. Bertrand thought he must be the lady's husband.

Everyone was brought to look at Bertrand. They all smiled and then got on with the salvage operations.

By noon, they had raised a makeshift hut. Everyone stopped work, gathered round and sang in Latin, looking cheerful. Obviously they now considered the monastery operational again. They had the smug look of a man who's managed to mend his central-heating by his own efforts.

Bertrand sat on, feeling lonelier and lonelier. The people who came to smile and pat him increasingly irritated him. Soon they came less often. Finally he got up, walked over to the lady, and gestured towards his boat.

They gathered on the shore to wave him goodbye. They even sang him some kind of hymn and wept. The departure of the hero … But he thought they were relieved to see him go; he was becoming an embarrassment.

Resurre sailed beneath him, slowly and comfortably. She would take him anywhere. But where did he want to go? Back to his mercurial wife, his daughters, his sharp-tongued stepson? Back to his university colleagues and a weary vista of admitting he'd been wrong? Unbearable. His old life was as much use as an old suit to a man who's put on two stone in weight. Familiar but unwearable.

There was only one place to go: Farne. Cuddy. They could fudge up some means of talking. They were both big intellects. His own Latin hadn't entirely gone. Oh, the books to be written! His colleagues would be green with envy …

It was then he saw the book, floating in the waves. A big leather cover, worked marvellously with interlacing scrolls. A clasp that glinted like a goldfish under water. It must have been part of the monastic library, washed away in the storm. A fit gift to bring the man on Farne.

He heaved-to, and scrambled forward, reaching down. The book was heavy. Could it be the famous Lindisfarne Gospels? No. Similar but not the same.

Too late he sensed the gust of wind from behind; saw the shadow of the sail swing. The spar cracked against the back of his head and he knew nothing.

XXVI

"All right, you can see her for half-an-hour," said Madeleine. "But cool it. She's whacked."

Beth was sitting up in bed, staring out of the window.

"Hallo."

"Hallo." She didn't look round. He settled on a hard wooden chair, easing his bruises as best he could.

"I keep thinking I can see *Resurre*," said Beth "But when I look properly she's not there. Only I can't see all of the sea from this window."

"I'll go out and look, every ten minutes."

"Thanks."

There was a long silence. Not uncomfortable, just long. One question kept coming into Michael's mind. He didn't want to worry her, spoil the being-together. But finally he said:

"Cuddy. What was he like? Did you *like* him?"

"I never saw him. But I could tell the birds adored him. And Sally loves him. Hasn't she told you about him?"

"No."

"No, she wouldn't. She'd be scared Daddy might hear. But she whispered to me, in bed. Honestly, she talks about him as if he was the old family donkey. She seems to have spent most of the time riding around the island on his back. And you know how *mucky* she was when we found her? Well, she got herself mucky on purpose, to be like him.

"He tried to play games to amuse her. Only he couldn't remember most of them properly. And those he could, he couldn't make her understand. Except one they played on the sand with stones. You know what it was? Hopscotch. All those hundreds of years and – *hopscotch*."

170

"Funny, him choosing her, a little girl, when he couldn't stand women."

"She saw him first. Remember Daddy saying little children have sharper eyes because their minds are empty? The older you get, the more you only see what you expect to see. We were all blind but Sally.

"And I think *she* chose *him*. There was one thing she wanted very much; her hand healed. I dread to think what misery that hand must have caused her. Why do people always think little children can't have big emotions?"

"But why did he take ten days to heal her?"

"He had to make her believe he could do anything. When he banished the ravens, when the seals brought back his book, they were like stepping-stones to belief. So when he sent her to fetch the big fish, something she knew she could only do with two good hands, she trusted him absolutely. She *believed*."

Another silence. But it wasn't in Michael's nature to be silent for long.

"But if he hated women, why'd he go for all you females? He ignored me."

"What did you ever want of him? Or *Resurre*?"

"A doss-around with the Vikings."

"I said *want*, Mike; not *whim*."

"O.K. So I wanted nothing of Cuddy. And I almost got it." He told her about Ross Links.

Beth nodded. "You see, there's a gap between Cuddy and us. He doesn't cross, to interfere with us. We have to go to him, and only a very strong desire will drive us across the gap: Sally wanting her hand whole; me wanting to save Daddy. You don't have that kind of want, Mike. You're pretty happy with your lot; self-sufficient."

"I wanted you back safe." Mike blurted it out without meaning to. Beth still didn't look at him, but a blush swept up from the neck of her pyjamas.

"Well, you got me back safe, didn't you?"

There was a moment's silence and then Beth said, "Please go and look for Daddy."

Mike fled, and stared out to sea. It was as Beth said. He kept seeing *Resurre* out of the corner of his eye, but when he looked straight, she vanished. As if she was only a few seconds away, poised on the brink of becoming. Or as if his eyes were playing tricks.

"Nothing," he said, flinging himself back in the chair. Another silence. He started an argument to break it. Only a little one, so as not to hurt her.

"O.K. But what about Madeleine? How come she got off so easy, after trampling on his tomb like that? Those women in the old books got struck dead, just for trespassing in the cathedral churchyard."

"I've thought about that. Cuddy cursed me, you know. Three times. Because I was naked, and he was delirious. But the curses sort of bounced off me. Oh, they threw me around. I still ache. But if I'd been thinking different thoughts, those curses would have killed me."

"What different thoughts?" Now he had her in complete disarray. Blushes came and went. Her eyes were everywhere.

"Well ... I was only naked by accident ... and only thinking about being cold and lonely and saving Daddy. I wasn't feeling seductive, and I wasn't *being* seductive. It's not females as such who upset Cuddy. I'm sure he always liked girl children. And holy abbesses could twist him round their little finger, getting him to prophesy the future and that sort of thing. But he'd turned his back on sex to be a monk and there are some women who'll go after any man they think's unattainable, even a dead saint. You'd have to be a woman to understand. They wanted to embarrass and corrupt him, to get power over him. They were the ones awful things happened to."

"Madeleine's pretty sexy."

"Yes, but that wasn't what she was after when she stepped on Cuddy's tomb. She didn't touch him as a man, but as something inexplicable and mysterious; like she wanted to touch the Dirty Bottles at Alnwick. Daddy's rationalism was choking her. She wanted help against being imprisoned in Daddy's world. It sounded like she was insulting Cuddy, but it was really a kind of noisy angry praying."

"And she got what she asked for"

"More; he took away her rage too. Cuddy gives you things you don't even know you need – that's why it's so painful at first. Ever seen a good gardener pruning roses? It's terrible – he cuts away nearly everything. You think he's killed them – till you see the way they bloom four months later."

"Yeah, painful," said Mike with feeling. "But Cuddy hasn't given you what you asked for yet."

Beth went so pale, he was sorry he'd said it.

"Not yet. But he's given me something. I loved Daddy the wrong way; because he was strong and clever and protected me. Like you might love a house that kept you warm and dry. When you mend the roof of that house – are you loving the house or yourself? Now I can see Daddy as he is, I can love him as he is.

"Besides, Cuddy said to me: *Femina bona es*. He wasn't flattering me. He was pointing out a fact; making me responsible for myself. So I couldn't cheat myself any more."

"So now you'll go straight into a nunnery."

"No. That was a daydream; my way of running away from Daddy … Madeleine … Sally … you. Cuddy didn't want me to be like *him* – but like myself. And I think I'm quite sexy, really."

"But why is Cuddy so violent? I thought saints were gentle and loving."

"Like Uncle Tom Hornsby?"

They both exploded into giggles. Uncle Tom was a Rotarian,

and worked at it. No one was allowed to pass him in the street without a smile and wave. He always asked how you were, and how your relatives were. Never forgot a birthday. Every time there was an earthquake disaster, Uncle Tom was in the local paper, organising raffles and donkey derbies. He raised hundreds of pounds. Everyone liked Uncle Tom – so why were they giggling?

"Uncle Tom pruning rose-trees!"

"Agonising over every leaf!"

They stopped at last, wiping their eyes.

"Dentists hurt," said Beth.

"Surgeons hurt," said Mike.

"Christ hurt people so much they crucified Him."

"But He didn't strike women dead."

"Oh, Mike." Beth leaned back against the pillow and he realised that laughing had exhausted her. She could hardly speak for weariness. "I can't solve all your problems. Cuddy never said he never sinned; he went on and on about how much he *had* sinned. Saints aren't people who never sin. Saints are people who love God so much He can't say no to them. And since saints can't say no to people, they become a kind of bridge. Like Cuddy …" Her eyes went to the ever-changing sea. "Cuddy …" she said again, "… the Wind Eye …"

But her voice trailed off and before Mike could speak her eyelids had closed and she was asleep.

He listened for a moment to her quiet breathing, then tiptoed out of the room and down the stairs. The kitchen was full of the smell of baking again:

Madeleine's way of keeping devils at bay. It worked pretty well, actually. He picked up a jam-tart and drifted to the window. The sea was still playing *Resurre*-tricks on the eye.

"Mum?"

"Ye–es?"

"What *is* a Wind Eye?"

Madeleine laughed. "Not you as well!"

"What do you mean?"

"Sally's been plaguing my life out about Wind Eyes. And it just so happens that I can tell you exactly what a Wind Eye is: a plain, simple, common-or-garden *window*."

"How do you know?"

"I have it here, in writing." She picked up an ancient pink dictionary. "WINDOW. *Derived from Icelandic* vindr *meaning* wind *and* auga *meaning* eye. Icelanders are direct descendants of the Norsemen. The old Norse for *window* is *wind eye*."

"But … but …"

"Oh, you have to understand what Norsemen's windows were like before you see the point. They didn't have any glass, or even oiled parchment, poor souls. Their windows were just holes in the wall, with wooden shutters across. So they had the choice of staying warm and snug in the dark, or opening up the window to see what was outside, and getting wet and frozen in the process."

"But I still don't see why they should call Cuddy the Wind Eye."

"Well, think of us driving up here from Cambridge, snug and warm, and in the dark about all kinds of things. Until we found *Resurre*. The Wind Eye's boat, those fishermen said. So you chose to sail *Resurre*, and you got cold and wet and you *saw* things. Right?"

"Yeah. I suppose so." But Mike felt cheated. He had liked the idea of the wind having eyes; of the whole sky over Farne being one great eye.

He shrugged, and picked up two more jam tarts. "I wonder which side of the Wind Eye Bertrand's on right now," he said, staring out at the restless, empty sea.

Bertrand came to, lying on his back. Overhead, *Resurre*'s mast circled gently against the late afternoon sky. The motion of the boat was like a cradle rocking. Little waves lapped alongside soothingly. He lay a long time, till his head stopped aching.

Then he sat up with a jerk. Farne dreamed in the sun a mile off. The lighthouse sat on its cliff above the carbide. The trip-boat from Seahouses was doing the rounds, with amplified commentary.

"... most famous as the home of St Cuthbert, who lived here in the seventh century. Those black-and-white ducks you see are still known as ..."

Bertrand scrambled into the stern and took hold of the sail. He hadn't willed himself back into the present day. He willed himself back into the seventh century.

No mist descended. Lighthouse, carbide and trip-boat persisted. Trippers waved to him. He did not wave back. An empty detergent-bottle tapped against *Resurre*'s bow.

Bertrand bent every ounce of his will. But he found he couldn't even move in space, let alone time. He and the detergent-bottle just bobbed around together; as *Resurre*'s sail swung back and forwards with every puff of wind. If anything, the gentle waves were bearing him towards Monk's Heugh beach. Without the steering-oar, he was helpless.

And felt pointless. He looked, for reassurance, at the wound in his shoulder. Dried by the sun, it was now no more than a scratch. Evidence of nothing. *Had* he saved a lady? *Had* he killed a man?

Was *Resurre* really a time-traveller? Or merely a haunted boat, a kind of psychic tape-recorder playing back memories of things that had happened to her? Or was the whole business a dream in the mind of the saint as he slumbered on Farne? Had Cuddy merely turned over in his sleep as the angry, questing minds of the Studdards disturbed him like buzzing flies on a hot summer day? Perhaps all three. Bertrand didn't know.

All he knew for sure was that, whatever it was, he was shut out from it now. Shut out, into a dry boring world where only things you could touch, smell and measure existed. Once that world had been his fortress. Now it was nothing but a tiny jail, full of day-trippers and detergent bottles.

It was unbearable.

A large motor-boat was approaching, full of men in bobble-caps and bristling with sea-fishing rods. It stopped, engine idling.

"Caught anything, mate?"

Bertrand's reply was unprintable, but lost in the noise of the engine.

"All right are you, mate?" Bertrand shouted something even ruder. But the men waved cheerily as their boat's engine roared, and they made off.

All afternoon the incoming tide took *Resurre* nearer home. By dusk, she was only a quarter of a mile off-shore. Bertrand saw smoke begin to trickle from the Monk's Heugh chimneys. A light went on in the kitchen.

Life was going on without him. But in another half hour, he knew, with absolute certainty, *Resurre* would gently and safely tip him onto his own beach; back into his old life.

It was still unbearable. He considered jumping into the sea, as a final gesture of defiance. But somehow he knew the waves would wash him ashore alive, just the same.

There was nothing to do but sit still, eyes shut, waiting for it to happen.

The trouble was, he was one of those people with a photographic memory. It was the basis of his success as a scholar. Pages of books began appearing before his closed eyes; and one book in particular. The Chronicles of Symeon, monk of Durham, read only the previous day. Still, it was a way of passing the time …

Then one page began repeating. It concerned the monks who had fled from Holy Island to Durham to escape the Viking invasion of 875, carrying the coffin of St Cuthbert.

Seven servants of the monks were privileged to bestow more close and constant attendance upon the holy body. Four, named Hunred, Edmund, Franco and Stitheard were of greater repute than the other three ... it is the boast of many persons in Northumbria that they are descended from one of these.

Stitheard.

Studdard.

There had to be a connection! The clue to everything that had happened lay there, if only he could find it.

There was only one way to find it. Resign his fellowship. Come to live at Monk's Heugh permanently. Comb the shores for evidence of Cuddy; collect and study every object he found. Sail *Resurre* winter and summer; and someday, somehow, slip through the time-curtain again and meet Cuddy face-to-face and never return to the dry-as-dust twentieth century.

Then he gasped. That was exactly what Uncle Henry had done before him ... and Uncle Henry's father before that. Studdards back to the dawn of time. Living in Monk's Heugh, guarding *Resurre*.

Twenty yards from shore, there was a thump for'ard. He looked up. Two black birds were sitting on the bow. They might have been ravens, but he couldn't be sure in the dusk. They had white objects in their beaks.

As he stood up, they flew off. But the white things fell to the deckboards with a soft thud. He picked them up.

They were greasy; lumps of primitive lard. As Mike would have said, Anglo-Saxon boot-polish.

It was a gift

It was an apology.

It was even quite a good joke.

Author's Note

I have used the word "Viking" in this book, though its use during the 7th century is nowhere recorded; everyone knows what a Viking is, and I refuse to use terms like "Norse sea-raider", which would enlighten no one and simply add to the length of the book.

Purists will also no doubt tell me that Holy Island was only sacked twice, in A.D. 793 and again in 875. However there is a folk-legend extant on the Northumbrian coast that St Cuthbert emerged one day from his cell on Farne, to see Vikings sacking his monastery on Holy Island. According to the legend, he cursed them. A great storm arose and the Vikings perished in their ships in Holy Island harbour, where the ships' ribs can still be seen on the sea-bed during exceptionally low tides.

I have chosen to use the legend, and not just because it makes a better story. Legends about St Cuthbert are important, because information about the saint can be found at three levels.

The top level, which might be termed ecclesiastical party-line, is found in church guide-books and dictionaries of saints. It depicts St Cuthbert as gentle, pious and a lover of bird and beast; very similar to many other plaster-saints.

When one consults the medieval chroniclers of Cuthbert's own church at Durham, however, a different picture emerges. Here is a saint as active in death as in life, who ruled his monastery with an iron hand from beyond or within the tomb. Who punished dishonest priors, thieving Danes, and even put a presumptuous William the Conqueror to flight. And however much rationalists will attempt to rationalise away such matters, it remains a fact that, of the three great churches which existed in the north just prior to the Danish invasions, one (Hexham) was totally destroyed by Danish skulduggery, and never regained more than parochial status. Another, York, was so reduced by the 10th century that for some years it could not even support a bishop. Only Cuthbert's Durham waxed prosperous during the years of invasion and chaos. By 1000 A.D., it owned much of what until recently was County Durham. The name of the area in the Conqueror's time was "St Cuthbertslond".

Below the level of the monastic chroniclers like Symeon and Reginald, remains a third layer, of folk-legend, which has never, as far as I know, been thoroughly recorded and collated. It would prove a rewarding task, if one had the time and patience, and the knack of getting the local people's confidence. Many of the legends are to do with St Cuthbert's provision of sanctuary for fugitives. Not only to criminals and political refugees at Durham itself. There is one tale of a hard-pressed stag gaining the churchyard of one of Cuthbert's churches, and mocking huntsmen and hounds alike before falling asleep in the church doorway. Even in more recent times St Cuthbert seems to have protected his cathedral against Nazi bombers. Mrs Kathleen Parker wrote to me: The raid was a Baedeker raid on the same pattern as those on the cathedrals of Exeter and Coventry. I was one of a group on fire-watching duty in the Cathedral Close that night. We saw anti-aircraft shells bursting high above the central tower of the cathedral in a clear sky. Suddenly the top of the tower disappeared in mist while we were still in moonlight. The mist had not come up from the river, it had just appeared. The plane dropped its bombs harmlessly in the riverside woods near Finchale about one-and-a-half miles in a direct line from the Galilee Chapel of the cathedral. The Observer Corps insisted there had been no smoke screens in the area that night so the protective mist has remained unexplained.

The Making of Me

A WRITER'S CHILDHOOD

Robert Westall

Edited by Lindy McKinnel

In his own words, the extraordinary childhood of one of the most influential children's authors of the twentieth century.

Robert Westall's writing draws much from his childhood. He grew up on Tyneside, the only child of two unusual people and the beloved grandson of eccentric grandparents. He was 10 when war broke out – a good age to enjoy it. War was exciting – Tyneside was heavily bombed and young Bob had to live through the terror of the air raids. These childhood experiences feature in many of his books.

Westall's upbringing and family life during the 1930s and 40s is vividly brought to life in *The Making of Me* – the character and expectations of his parents and grandparents, the influences of his surroundings, the brutality of school life and what it meant in his peer group to be both short-sighted and fat. Here are all the influences that were later to surface in his writings.

As a writer, Robert Westall had the rare gift of combining literary excellence with an immense talent for capturing the imagination and interest of children. He wrote over 50 novels, including twentieth-century classics *The Machine Gunners*, *The Kingdom by the Sea*, *Blitzcat* and *The Scarecrows*. He was twice awarded the Carnegie Medal and also received the Guardian Award and the Smarties Prize.

The Making of Me is essential reading for anyone who wants to understand this unique and imaginative writer.

Westall's 'narrative power never fails'

TES

'Fascinating scenes from Westall's childhood, and insights into the development of a fine writer. A lovely book.'

David Almond

'Provides ample reminders of all the force and honesty that went into his work'

Nicholas Tucker, Books for Keeps

Catnip Books
ISBN 10: 1 84647 008 0
ISBN 13: 978-1-84647-008-0
216 pp
£7.99